PENGUIN BOOKS

COMES THE NIGHT

Hollis Hampton-Jones studied German and French in Berlin, Salzburg, Vienna and Paris, where she was swept briefly into the modelling world. She worked in theatre in New York City, and now lives in Nashville. She is the author of the novel *Vicious Spring*.

Comes the Night

HOLLIS HAMPTON-JONES

PENGUIN BOOKS

Published by the Penguin Group
Penguin Books Ltd, 80 Strand, London WC2R ORL, England
Penguin Group (USA) Inc., 375 Hudson Street, New York, New York 10014, USA
Penguin Group (Canada), 90 Eglinton Avenue East, Suite 700, Toronto, Ontario,
Canada M4P 2Y3 (a division of Pearson Penguin Canada Inc.)
Penguin Ireland, 25 St Stephen's Green, Dublin 2, Ireland
(a division of Penguin Books Ltd)
Penguin Group (Australia), 250 Camberwell Road, Camberwell, Victoria 3124, Australia
(a division of Pearson Australia Group Pty Ltd)
Penguin Books India Pvt Ltd, 11 Community Centre,
Panchsheel Park, New Delhi – 110 017, India
Penguin Group (NZ), 67 Apollo Drive, Rosedale, Auckland 0632, New Zealand
(a division of Pearson New Zealand Ltd)
Penguin Books (South Africa) (Pty) Ltd, 24 Sturdee Avenue,
Rosebank, Johannesburg 2196, South Africa

Penguin Books Ltd, Registered Offices: 80 Strand, London WC2R ORL, England

www.penguin.com

First published 2011
1

The moral right of the author has been asserted

Set in 12/18pt Bembo Book MT Std
Typeset by Jouve (UK), Milton Keynes
Printed in Great Britain by Clays Ltd, St Ives plc

ISBN: 978-0-241-14224-0

www.greenpenguin.co.uk

To Herbert, Deirdre and Logan, with profound
gratitude for their love, patience and support

Vienne la nuit sonne l'heure
Les jours s'en vont je demeure.

Comes the night, sounds the hour,
The days go by but I remain.

from 'Le Pont Mirabeau',
Guillaume Apollinaire (1880–1918)

We shared a womb, floated around in there together, grew fingers and toes, sucked each other's thumbs, developed hearts, lungs and brains. He was out of there first, kicked and pushed his way through, but I had a hard time getting out. The umbilical cord was wrapped around my neck, so every time I tried to escape, the noose tightened.

The doctor, who was an Italian, sang an aria while he squeezed my head with his forceps, yanked me out and sliced the cord.

I didn't cry.

Even when they hung me upside down.

Nurse's finger in my throat cleared the airway.

Ah . . . breath! Life! And a brother.

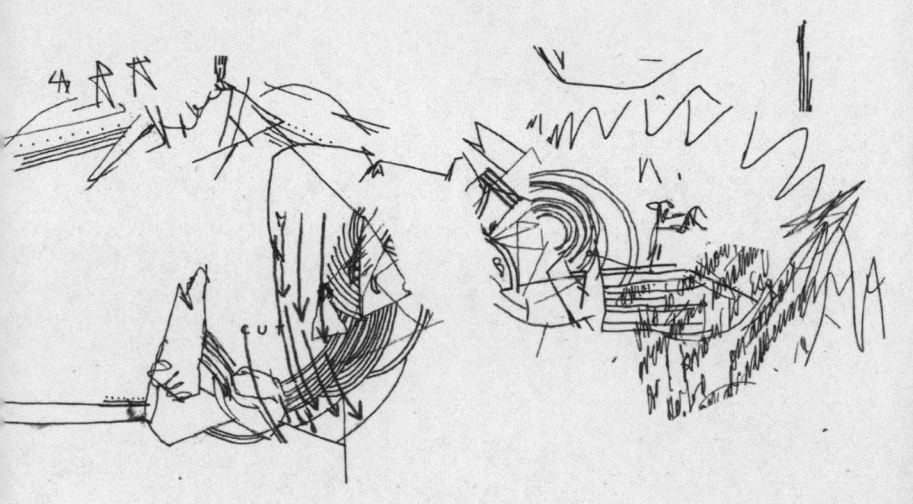

A lot of people have a hard time breathing in Nashville.

Topographically Nashville is a bowl, which means everything just sits inside of it and rots. The air is thick with particles of all kinds. Probably if you looked at the air through a microscope, each square inch would contain a secret battalion of monstrous, fuzzy creatures.

It's good to be away from the monsters.

We shared a womb, we shared a crib, we shared a room, we shared a house, and now we're sharing an apartment, this one in Paris, paid for by all the recreated noses, the implant-stuffed breasts, the fat-suctioned thighs – our father's Frankensteined parade that wanders the health-food stores, the shopping malls, the country clubs, the wine emporiums of Nashville.

The apartment was decorated by Mom with mostly Napoleonic antiques. There's a marble-topped table with four sphinxes for legs, and a daybed upholstered with gold bees. But these are not the most noticeable things in the room, because they're obscured by all the stuff that Ben Ho gathers: farming tools, sheet metal, a window frame with one pane missing, seven old dial telephones, each weighing about twenty-five pounds, signs with peeling letters, anything with red plastic, Czech and Russian matchboxes, and piles of illustrated medical books of varied outdatedness.

On the sphinx-supported table between us sits a cake. I stare into his eyes, at the nineteen miniature flames burning in each of them, until we close our eyes and blow out the candles. Of course the cake is chocolate. My tongue decodes the butter, the eggs, the Belgian chocolate folded in. The flour, the sugar, the baking soda.

'So, what do you have for me, Meade?'

He gets his present first because he was born first.

I hand him my box. I used his calligraphy pens to write 'To Bennett Horatio Harden IV' on it. My calligraphic skills suck compared to his, but I know he'll love what's inside.

Inside is some antique accounting paper, thick and yellowed, with some crazy, cramped handwriting on it. Maybe this blue ink list of expenses is all that's left of this person.

'Wow. Thanks.' His eyes shine. Then he finds the old brown Oxford-style shoes. Maybe they once belonged to the accountant. And below that, the heavy, smooth-handled, rusted axe.

He turns it over in his hand, examines the blade. I can tell he's really touched. He arranges the axe and the shoes carefully on the fireplace mantle.

Then he gives me my present. It's the kind of mobile that you might hang over a crib, but this one has little drawings and paintings of his clipped on to it with clothespins.

'That's so cool.' Something to stare at, lying on my bed, a place to go.

Then it's time for our birthday dance. We sing 'Happy Birthday to Us' as loud as we can, while I hold on to him, and he flings me around the room in a sort of demented waltz.

On the outside, he's dark and I'm light, but on the inside, it's the other way around.

* * *

I wake up full of hatred towards alarm clocks and champagne.

I feel like my head is trailing behind my body, lolling around like an infant's with no neck muscles, as I make my way to the kitchen. I fill the espresso pot with water and coffee, put it on the stove, and wait for the gurgling sound.

It's a mercifully grey morning.

On the kitchen counter are four empty champagne bottles and a full ashtray.

Ben Ho doesn't have any classes until this afternoon, so he gets to sleep it off. I pour myself some water and take French hangover medicine: paracetamol with codeine. Then I take my Adderall. The coffee starts bubbling upwards.

I empty the ashtray before I light a cigarette. It really bothers me to start the day with yesterday's butts.

When I glance at the window frame, the ceiling beams, or anything with an edge, for a split second I see a thin blue neon light tracing its side.

* * *

The blue neon light keeps reappearing, on Chef Gaillard's big silver knife blade as he chops at high speed, and then around the rim of the copper sautéing pan, like a planetary ring.

In this culinary world I wear a white uniform, so bright that I can hardly look at it. Bleached by the Ritz launderers here at the Ritz Escoffier School, my Dad-sponsored option to be in Paris with Ben Ho. It takes me a while to pin up all my hair to fit it under my toque. It makes my head feel heavy. Marie Antoinette's head must have felt like this.

I imagine her coiffed head falling into a wooden bucket.

Chef Gaillard is prising an oyster from its shell. I wonder what an oyster does inside its shell all day. What kind of life would that be? To be just a wriggling grey lump?

The students around me, mostly Japanese, are watching very intently.

I can't do that when there are so many things to look at.

The nostril on the guy next to me, that flexes slightly when he breathes, for instance. Jostling its blue neon frame out of existence.

★ ★ ★

After class I turn in my uniform for its voyage to the laundry, and then I find my favourite bathroom, off the lobby. It's nearly always empty.

The perfect place. So clean. My hair is still pinned up, out of the way. I get down on my knees and touch the back of my throat, the little fleshy tail that hangs down in there. And then it emerges:

ENTRÉE CHAUDE

cream

butter

vin blanc de Bourgogne

oysters and their liquid

salmon roe

shallots

chives

fennel

bile

Whitish and thick. I wipe one fleck from the toilet seat. It's such a relief to flush. And then it's just water. Clear, pure water on cool porcelain.

At the sink I rinse my mouth and take some deep breaths. I avoid looking at myself in the mirror. I just concentrate on my hands as I wash them.

* * *

When I walk out on to the street, there's a heavy rain coming down, the heaviest I've seen since I've been in Paris, which seems to get a lot of drizzle. This is a much more emphatic rain.

Most people walking are clutching black umbrellas, manoeuvring themselves around each other's shelter. Some people just have hats. The hatless and the umbrella-less stand clustered under awnings, smoking cigarettes.

I fall into the hatless and umbrellaless category, but it's warm out, so I don't mind being wet. I start walking in a state of wet-acceptance, and it makes me feel free. Once you accept rain, everyone else looks ridiculous dodging it. I head towards the Seine so I can watch water on water.

With each step, my hair, my T-shirt, my jeans, my sneakers, are more densely soaked. The jeans start to feel heavy around my legs. Drops fall off my eyelashes and run down my face, as if I were crying.

What if, when you cried, tears came out of all the pores of your body and soaked you like this? My arms would cry, my fingertips, my stomach. Tears would pool in my belly button.

'She doesn't have enough sense to come in out of the rain,' I hear my father's voice say.

When I get to the Seine I stop for a moment on the *quai* and look down at the river. Grey-green water rushing so that it makes me dizzy. I have this weird urge to jump into it, and I can almost feel my body being swept along in the current, kicking my jeans-heavy legs hard to try to avoid the eddies that would crash me into the bridge.

I start to feel queasy. I turn away and walk, faster now. A woman glances disapprovingly at me from beneath her umbrella. Her little world is covered in paisley.

She can't see the massive dark cloud swooping over us, or all the statues weeping from the tops of buildings.

★ ★ ★

When I get back to the Marais and walk up the stairs to our apartment, my sneakers make farting noises all the way. There's a trail of wet shoeprints behind me. Centuries of shoes have left their marks on this staircase and worn it thin on the centre of each step.

Ben Ho's not home, but he left me a note: 'Meet me at Café du Passage at 6.' With one of the smiley face characters that he draws. Just a few extra lines, but they have personality. This one looks crazed and jeering.

Ben Ho is not a big user of his cellphone, which is hard for me. He likes to be unreachable sometimes. Lots of times.

'Reality interrupters,' he calls them.

I drip all the way to the bathroom and peel off my wet

clothes. I'm starting to feel chilled, so I run a bath. I add lavender essence to the water. Lavender is supposed to be calming.

The bathtub is so long and deep that I can almost float in it, and I'm nearly six feet tall. I like the feeling of my buoyancy, and the shift of soundscape when my ears are submerged: from the treble line of the water from the spigot hitting the surface, to the bass line of its impact below, amplified by the porcelain walls.

After I've floated around for a while, dried off and combed out my hair, I decide to inspect myself in the mirror.

There's no full-length mirror, so to see my whole body, I have to stand on top of the toilet.

Even though it's a gruesome sight, some perverse part of me can't resist looking. I stare at my mirror-person and I can see through her skin to the thickly flowing, gelatinous yellow rivers of fat beneath. I could fill hundreds of oil lamps with it, I could light a ballroom with my fat supplies, the lamps glowing, burning; the golden, airy, high-ceilinged room reeking of me, of the fat of other animals I've consumed, of the cow fat hiding in the oyster appetizer I just ate, the wetsuit of fat of the oyster itself.

I stand up straight, square my shoulders, and hold my stomach in. Mom always tells me I'm too thin, but I think she just wants me to be fatter than she is.

I step off the toilet and stand closer to the mirror. What most people notice about me is my hair. It's light blonde, and it hangs down to my waist. People like to touch it, sometimes people I don't even know, and when they do, they usually say something about it being very soft. But to me it's just normal, not really that special.

I like Ben Ho's wild, dark hair. You can grab a hunk of it and make a shape out of it, and it will stay like that for a while.

We look nothing alike, except that we're both tall. When we were eleven, I was a little taller, but now he has four inches on me. I wish we were identical twins, and that I could look at the world through his serene, dark eyes.

Sometimes I don't really feel things until I tell Ben Ho about them. Then he'll lock those eyes on mine, and as I look into them and talk, I can see my own emotions reflected there. Like his eyes are actually the windows of my soul.

When we were fourteen and I found Mom OD'd on

Xanax and wine and had to call 911, I didn't feel it until I told him about it. Things like that.

But there are some things I don't tell him. Like the throwing-up thing. Or how every once in a while, when I'm alone, I still suck my thumb.

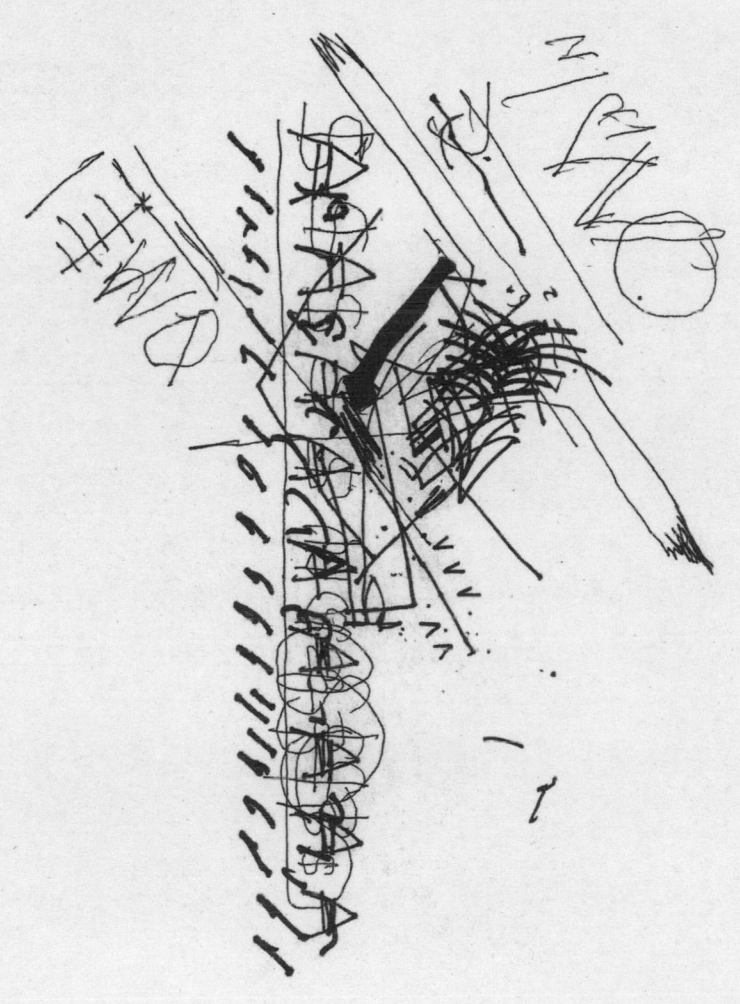

I want a hash cigarette really badly, to help settle my stomach.

I don't know why queasiness makes me sweat. My face is hot, and I feel twin rivers of sweat running down the sides of my body.

At least I can have a glass of wine soon, and smoke a regular cigarette, when I meet Ben Ho at Café du Passage. If I can make it through this Métro ride to Bastille, smelling everyone else's sweat.

I try not to sway. I'm free-floating, though, in the middle of a pack of people with no handrail available to me, just trying to gauge the rhythm of the starting and stopping.

I bump lightly into a guy in an orange shirt. His sweat smells tangy. He steadies me with his large hand.

I take a deep breath and try not to let my claustrophobia overcome me in this crowd. But when I breathe in, I taste the throng.

People are loud today. It almost seems like they all know each other, like I'm the only one who doesn't belong.

I burst out of the doors at Bastille, but so does the crowd. As I surface I find that I'm entering an even bigger crowd. There seems to be some kind of event going on.

Police are stationed everywhere. They're wearing a different uniform than any I've seen before. They look like Ninja Turtles with black shells.

I squeeze through clusters of people. I think this is a demonstration of some sort.

Maybe I can find some hash.

I try to make my way to the café, but it's like this mob is some organism that I'm stuck inside of, and I can only move in the direction that the organism is moving.

Which makes me panicky.

I look around to figure out what's going on. People are chanting on megaphones, but I can't make out what they're saying.

I see signs that say BUSH EST TERRORISTE. I notice a dark-haired girl who's wearing a T-shirt that says BU(LL)SH(IT).

What if the mob discovers that I'm an American? Would they hate me if they knew?

But I didn't vote for him.

Actually, I didn't vote. But I wouldn't have voted for him.

Somebody's smoking hash. That smell I love.

I'm almost at the rue de Charonne when a voice screams right next to my right ear: 'LES AMERICAINS SONT LES COCHONS DU MONDE!'

I look at the screamer's face. The veins are bulging on his temples. He has a scar above one eye. His eyes are black. He pumps his fist in the air with a wiry, dark-skinned arm.

For a moment I think he's going to punch me, but I keep walking.

I reach into my purse and feel for my smallest bottle. I can take Xanax without water, because it's such a tiny pill.

I swallow. In about fifteen minutes the crowd won't matter any more.

* * *

When I walk into the café, I'm relieved to see that Ben Ho is already there.

'Hey,' he says. He does a brief headlock manoeuvre on me. 'Pretty crazy out there, huh?'

'People hate us.' I take a sip of his red wine.

'Oh, they don't hate us. Don't take everything so personally. You want some wine?'

'Sure.'

We sit down at a table by the bar, and as I sip my wine and concentrate on his calmness, I start to feel better.

Also the Xanax kicks in.

* * *

I probably should have tried to stand up before we drank the second bottle. Now I really have to pee, and standing up is a challenge. I hold on to the edges of the table and raise myself a few inches off my chair, but it's too much too fast. When I drop back down my chair seems to be in a different position. I just manage to catch the edge of it, and it see-saws to the side. Ben Ho's arm stops me from falling.

'Are you okay?'

I try to find his eyes. There they are. They don't look serene any more.

'I have to pee.'

'Well, go pee.'

'Can you help me get up?'

He pops out of his chair so easily. 'I told you, you should have eaten something.'

Goose liver. He was eating goose liver. I try to push this nauseating thought out of my mind. Don't look at the empty terrine. Don't look at it.

Fat, honking things. Force-fed. Tubes in their beaks.

I feel Ben Ho's arm wrap around my chest as he uses his leverage to lift me up out of my chair. I try to move my feet in time as he propels me towards the bathroom. I concentrate on the floor. Left foot. Right foot. Left foot. Right.

The wood floor changes into tile.

'Hold on to the sink,' he says. I obey. I find myself in the mirror. I see my blonde hair. The door closes. Ben Ho is on the outside. I'm on my own.

It's a tiny bathroom. I can do this. I unzip my jeans and pivot myself around to the toilet. I land a little heavily on the seat, but I'm safe. Just in time. I release a litre's worth of pee.

I'm lighter now.

Ben Ho bangs on the door. 'Are you okay?'

'I'm fine.' I lean my head against the cool plaster wall.

'Meade!'

'Fine.' The wall feels good.

The door swings open and Ben Ho's in the bathroom with me. He closes the door behind him, holds my face by my chin and examines my eyes. 'So what did you take?'

'I'm all right.'

'Well stand up and pull your pants up, then.'

I get the giggles.

'Come on, Meade, get up. Let's get you out of here.'

I spin back around towards the sink. The sink is my friend. Very sturdy. I pull myself up. The only problem is my pants. Bending down to pull them up is a challenge that might be beyond me.

I feel my panties slide magically up my legs. Then my jeans. The zipper. The button. His hands.

'Why are you always taking those fucking pills?'

'I was anxious.'

'Well, you're in really great shape now. So much better. Now come on. Help me out here. Let's walk.'

I feel my legs again. They seem to be working better now. I only have to lean on him a little, against the pulsating wires of his electric-fence arms, and I manage to smile at the waiter as we pause while Ben Ho puts money in his hand.

* * *

The taxi ride is nice, when the door closes us off from the street, and it's quiet. The interior is black. Ben Ho lets me lie down with my head on his lap. I feel his thigh bone against my cheek. He doesn't say anything. The car is heavy and smooth on the road. After a while, Ben Ho picks up a strand of my hair and winds it absently around his finger, and for the rest of the drive he rubs the ends of it back and forth against his cheek, which is why I've always had long hair.

I feel so light. When we get home, my legs are cooperating, or maybe not even necessary. I float up the stairs.

The next thing I know, I'm in bed, alone, watching the mobile that dangles above my head.

It moves, almost imperceptibly, but it's not spinning.

* * *

When I throw up in the morning, the recipe is simple:

vin de Bordeaux
Xanax

I don't think I can handle sauce day at school. Too many eggs involved. I go back to sleep.

When I wake up, bars of sunlight stripe my bed, forming a jail of light. I break out of my cell.

As I head towards the kitchen, I'm assaulted by a breakfast smell.

'Ben Ho?' I call out, but there's no answer.

In the kitchen I see the breakfast he's left for me. Or the anti-breakfast, rather.

Two cold fried eggs sitting on a plate. He's cut the whites neatly so that they're shaped like eyes. And he must have raided my pill supply. In the middle of each yolk, he's placed a blue Adderall as a pupil. He's taken one, two, three, four . . . sixteen of the oblong-shaped Xanax and planted them into the whites along the top and bottom, so that they're sticking out like eyelashes. Emerging from the right eye is one Vicodin tear, half dissolved and brown. He must have soaked the Vicodin in coffee.

Nineteen total. Fuck. I'm going to have to hide my pills from him. I take one more look at the stomach-turning eyes to try to figure out how to salvage the pills in a way that doesn't involve touching the disgusting eggs. A fork? No. I need something with more surgical precision, so I go into the bathroom and rummage through my make-up bag.

Tweezerman comes to the rescue. I force myself to go back to the eyes, lay out a clean, folded dish cloth next to them and, plucking out each pill carefully, I place them one by one on the cloth. I'm able to wipe the bits of egg white off of the Xanax. The Adderall I have to give a quick rinse to get rid of the congealed yolk. I use the tweezers to hold them under the flow of water from the sink and then swallow them before they dissolve any more. Only the Vicodin tear is unsalvageable, and I mourn the loss with tears of my own as I scrape the remains on the plate into the trash.

* * *

I stay in the apartment all day. Sometimes I can't bear to go out in the streets, to walk around and feel like everything around me is muffled and distant, like I'm moving through projected images with a soundtrack. It's just one of those days when nothing seems real. I hold a pen or a glass, and I have to run my fingers along their surfaces to convince myself that they exist.

I trim my fingernails with my teeth.

I smoke sixteen cigarettes.

When Ben Ho comes home, he gives me a long head-lock and asks me if I want to go foraging with him, so I know he's not mad at me any more.

The V of his arm around my neck feels very real. Everything in the room snaps back into existence.

* * *

People throw away chairs. Perfectly good chairs that you can still sit on. At least people who live on the Seine with a view of the Eiffel Tower do.

Ben Ho and I stop to examine them. Two chairs with rounded backs in a light-coloured wood. Caning intact. Red velvet cushions.

'A throne for each of us,' he says. He picks up one, and I pick up the other. They're lightweight thrones.

'Wait!' he says, and I think he sees another treasure, so I set down my chair, but then he kneels down to tie my shoe. He gives it a double bow and then springs back up.

'Thanks.' I hadn't even realized that it was untied.

When we get to the Bir-Hakeim Bridge, we put our chairs by a golden statue of a giant mounted woman.

We light cigarettes. The woman and her horse are on the verge of jumping into the river.

'I see her galloping along the Seine and jumping all the bridges.'

'Good night for it,' says Ben Ho.

There's a big orange full moon hanging low in the sky. Maybe she can land there after she clears all the bridges.

'This place is silly beautiful,' he adds.

He'd be just as happy looking at a chain-linked lot filled with piles of smashed-up cars.

Or a hole in a brick with a spider inside of it.

But right now we're happy on our matching thrones.

It must be right on the hour, I'm not sure which hour, but the Eiffel Tower starts flashing, doing its glitter light show.

Which seems to get Ben Ho doing his monkey squawks.

I watch a group of people in black clothes hurry on by us. Obviously not monkey lovers.

'They're all monkeyists. Monkeyists, every one of them.' He jumps up on to his trash throne and squawks louder. The people walk faster.

I wait for him to pound his chest.

Three seconds.

It's very satisfying to feel his impulses and watch them be carried out.

I know exactly when he's going to quit his squawking and sit back down and light another cigarette.

After a few silent puffs, Ben Ho tosses his butt into the river and says, 'Come on. Let's go over to the studio.'

Which I was not expecting. He never invites me there.

We're the only people in the Métro who have red velvet seats. An unsmiling woman with magnified eyes stares at us as Ben Ho takes a picture of the inside of my mouth.

* * *

We carry our thrones up the winding stairs of the École des Beaux-Arts. You can still feel monks walking slowly around this place, from when it was a monastery. I wonder how they like the graffiti.

'What are you going to do with these?' I ask as we pass by the painters' studio. I glance inside, where the painters are silent as monks, meditating over their paintbrushes.

'Siamese twins.'

'Huh?'

'You'll see.'

When we get to the sculptors' studio, I'm suddenly overwhelmed by the beating of my heart, I have such a strong sense of it whooshing blood through my body. I feel like I'm inside myself, caught in the current of blood, dizzy from it, scared of crashing into bones.

'What's the matter? Go on in.' Ben Ho nudges me from behind with his chair.

I think the monks avoid this room. The sculptors are noisy. Drinking whisky and listening to gypsy music, banging shapes into things. They're all guys.

Except one girl, who walks straight up to Ben Ho and kisses him on the lips. Her hands are covered in clay, and she leaves a handprint on his shoulder.

She has long skinny legs and short dark hair, and she says, 'Where've you been?'

Where've you been. As if he should be reporting into her, or something. I instantly dislike her. She has one of those California-girl TV-show kind of voices that makes me want to kick her in her neat little row of teeth.

She looks at me with eyes rimmed in black eyeliner that comes to points on each side.

Ben Ho says, 'Linda, this is my twin, Meade.'

She holds out her cracked clay hand and kisses my

cheeks as if she were French. 'Hard to believe you guys are twins.' She crinkles her nose. 'You look so different.'

'Yeah. Well, we are.' I walk past her, which might seem rude, but at least she still has her teeth.

My heart is slam dancing inside me. I sit down next to a guy with a goatee and wire-rimmed glasses who is tinkering with a mechanical sculpture. He picks up a screwdriver and says, 'Want a whisky?'

'Sure.' Slow down, heart, please slow down.

He sloshes some into a semi-clean glass and hands it to me. 'I'm Jean-Marc. You're Ben's sister?'

The whisky rolls down my throat and coats my heart in a woolly blanket. 'Twin sister.'

'Oh, right. He told me he had a twin. Cheers.' He holds up his glass, which is smudged with grease.

'Cheers.' This time I just sip. 'What'd he say about me?'

'Not so much. He completely failed to tell me how shockingly beautiful you are.'

I can hardly see his eyes through his glasses. 'Your glasses are really dirty.'

Ben Ho is buzzing around the room, gathering tools. The California chick sits down and squeezes a hunk of clay.

'I can still see pretty well.' He takes off his glasses,

though, and wipes them on his T-shirt. His eyes are kind of swampy green. 'So, you're a Nashville girl?'

'Yeah. How about you? You're French?'

'Swiss. I'm from Geneva. A very boring city. Full of banks.'

'What are you making?'

'Here. I'll show you. Press this button.'

I press a big blue button, which releases a metal ball that rolls along tracks until it knocks a hammer, drops on to a springboard and spins a wheel that makes a pair of dentures clack open and shut, so that it gnaws on a bone.

I laugh, but it's kind of gross. The bone looks rancid, and I can't tell what kind of bone it is. 'What's the point of that?'

'To make you laugh. You see? It worked.'

We pull out cigarettes simultaneously, like duelling pistols. They're the same brand, Marlboro. He lights mine for me. I take a puff and watch Ben Ho.

He's sawing off the legs of my throne. I can tell it's mine, because there's an ink stain almost in the shape of a heart on the cushion. The whisky climbs back up my throat as I watch the amputation and the legs clank on to the floor.

The music gets louder and faster, and some of the sculptors dance whiskyly around the studio.

This Linda wraps her dirty, bony arms around Ben Ho and tries to get him to start dancing. He leans into her and says something close to her ear. She backs off. Ben Ho pulls out a razor and begins slicing at my cushion. Then he reaches into some of the incisions and pulls out tufts of the stuffing. The hair of dead horses.

My face is hot. I drink some more whisky. Jean-Marc says something to me, but I can't hear him over the din of pumped blood in my ears. I feel like I'm drowning in sound. His face is very close to mine. His mouth is making the shape of an 'o'. A life ring. I press my mouth against his. He drops his screwdriver. He sucks me out of my drowning. As I wrap my arms around his neck, he lifts me on to his lap.

When I come up for a breath, I watch Ben Ho hammer a long nail into the legless chair, twisted now on its side, connecting it with the arm of the undamaged one. His.

* * *

More music. More whisky. The clay chick gives Ben Ho a small clay army. I watch him tenderly wrap the soldiers in newspaper. One of the newspaper sheets has a photo of a guy who's about to be beheaded by some black-hooded people. The only skin showing on them is their hands.

This guy starts trying to kiss me, and I can't quite remember for a moment why I'm sitting on his lap. 'Come home with me,' he says into my ear, but Ben Ho is pulling me off of the guy's lap.

'Come on. Let's go.'

I see the clay chick's head hovering behind him. She's looking at me. She has a really stupid smile on her face.

I'm on my feet now. I'm taller than she is. Better reach for punching.

'She's not coming with us, is she?'

The smile disappears. She says something that I can't hear to Ben Ho, but he shakes his head. No! Ha!

We're walking fast. Down the winding stairs, through the courtyard, out the gate.

'Why were you making out with that guy? You don't even know him.'

'Now I do.'

'Yeah? What's his name?'

'Jean-Paul.'

'Jean-Marc!'

'Jean-Marc.'

'Did you have to be so rude to Linda?'

We step on to a wooden walking bridge. There's a bride and groom posing for pictures. Her dress billows in the wind.

'I can't believe you cut off the legs. My throne.'

He doesn't say anything, but he throws his long arm around me so that his hand drapes off of my shoulder. We pass the bride and groom. Their matrimonial smiles begin to tremble, waiting for the flash.

* * *

Not exactly spinning, but, you know, drunk, lying on my bed. Floating.

Remembering Dad drinking. Bloody Marys on a Sunday afternoon at the Club. Sun-reddened from golf. In the golf outfit. Yeah. Ben Ho and I are sipping Shirley Temples. I'm studying Dad's companion as I eat my maraschino cherry. A man in a woman's tennis outfit.

A cross-dressing Bloody Mary drinker.

After church. Released from my Sunday-school wear. A discarded smocked dress on my bed. Patent-leather shoes kicked into the corner. While Mom naps.

Ben Ho and I smelling of chlorine. Wet hair and khaki pants. After many trips down the blue slide, landing in the water.

The silence beneath the surface. Ahhh . . .

★ ★ ★

I get up early and go out to buy fresh croissants for me and Ben Ho. Inside the bakery, the quiet line of sleepy people is almost like Communion as we wait our turn for bread. Instead of swinging urns of frankincense, there's the wafting from the ovens.

By the time Ben Ho is up, I've squeezed oranges and made *café au lait*. I put two croissants on a plate together, curling in towards each other.

When he eats, I see pleasure in his eyes, a soft lamp in them that he turns on sometimes.

'There's a party on a barge tonight, if you want to go?' he says. He wets his finger to pick up some crumbs from the plate.

'That sounds fun.'

'Yeah. Should be.'

He doesn't say much else. He's not much of a morning talker.

When he leaves, I have a moment of panic over butter. All those layers and layers of butter brushed on to each thin sheet of dough. Fat. The fat of a cow making its way to my buttery thighs, my doughy hips. I wash my hands, get my finger ready.

But I decide to let it stay inside me, the warm croissant, and just pay penance for the rest of the day.

The rest of the day shall be fatless.

This Tunisian girl from Ben Ho's school is wearing a white dress, a wedding dress, but she's not getting married. She and a guy named Rolf are celebrating the five-year anniversary of their first kiss.

And they're demonstrating. I watch them kiss. Everyone watches them kiss, and a belly dancer circles around them clacking the tiny cymbals on her fingers.

Her stomach looks like it's having convulsions.

There's no one on this barge who I want to kiss. No one I want to taste.

Ben Ho and I are drinking champagne, which as far as kissing flavours go, is a pretty good one.

The couple goes from kissing to dancing.

Ben Ho really likes to dance. He's an extremely good dancer. He looks at me and takes my glass from me, sets it down. I know how to follow his lead.

I let my body be loose. I let him take me in his arms,

and it's as if I'm on a ride, being thrown this way and that, spun, folded. I'm hanging over his arm like a towel on a rack. Upside down, I notice the paned glass roof with squares of starry sky. A flash of a camera imprints itself on my vision, jumping and finally fading. The dance floor sways on the water. Up again and there's the shore, spinning. Spinning Louvre, spinning bridge.

People are watching us. People from desert places who ululate when they get excited. Vibrating tongues, and still the little clacking cymbals.

When the song ends I lean on Ben Ho's shoulder for a moment so I don't get dizzy.

Then he hands my champagne glass back to me. I steady myself in his eyes. We knock our glasses together and drink the soft bubbles. He burps.

'Nice, Ben Ho.'

'I can do better.'

'Spare me.'

He spots a light switch that excites him and goes off to take a picture. In his pictures, he makes the most mundane thing, like a pilot light, or a water bottle, look like its own universe.

I light a hash cigarette. The smell of it will bring him

back to me. I count seconds in my head. I'm betting on thirteen.

At seven, some guy comes up to me. 'So, you like to dance?'

I wave my cigarette. 'I'd rather smoke right now.'

'No, I'm not asking if you would like to dance with me. I'm asking, do you like to dance?' He lights a cigarette too.

He has beautiful dark eyes that reflect light. I can see the bar-side sconces in them. His shoes reflect light, too. They're catching the shimmers of the disco ball. 'Oh, yeah. Well, sometimes.'

Ben Ho seems to be fascinated with a sink now. Maybe the smoke's not going in the right direction. I lost count, but I'm sure it's way past thirteen.

'You and your boyfriend looked like you were really having fun. I took some pictures, if you want to see?'

'He is not my boyfriend!'

'No?'

'He's my twin.' And his twin alert must have gone off, because suddenly he's next to me, the sink abandoned, and he's taking the cigarette from between my fingers and inhaling as he scrutinizes the dark-eyed stranger.

Who is scrolling through the images on his camera. He finds one and shows it to me. I'm upside down and laughing. Ben Ho is cropped. Part of his shirt is a backdrop. My hair almost touches the floor.

Ben Ho trades me cigarette for camera. He looks at a few shots.

'These are good,' he says, handing the camera back to the guy.

The guy sort of bows his head. He smiles while his head is lowered. 'Thank you.'

'You want a hit?' I hold the hash cig out to him.

'Why not?' He partakes.

'Are you a photographer?' asks Ben Ho.

He holds on to his inhalation for a moment, and exhales, 'I am.'

'What kind of stuff do you do?' I like how Ben Ho asks a lot of questions when strangers talk to me.

'Fashion.' He looks at me. 'Are you with an agency?'

'What kind of agency?'

'You're not here to model?'

'Model? No, no. I'm in cooking school.'

'Ahhh. You want to be a chef?' He tilts his head and looks like he's about to laugh.

And it is pretty funny, really. Me, a chef. 'Well, it's not going all that well. I'm failing at sauces. I'm on the verge of being a cooking-school dropout. But I'm liking Paris.'

The river, the lights, the bridges, the hash are a very good combination. The surround-sound languages. I slip the cigarette from his fingers. Long, golden-skinned fingers. A delicate grasp.

Another puff for me.

The fingers remove a card from his wallet. 'My name is Majid. Give me a call if you're interested in doing some modelling. I think you could work here. I can help you find an agent.'

'Yeah, right.' He must not have noticed my fat thighs.

'You probably have many men say this to you. But I am quite serious. Just think about it. What is your name?'

'Meade.'

'Meade. Pleased to meet you.' He kisses my hand. No one has ever done that to me before. The kiss travels shiveringly up my arm. 'And you?'

'I'm Ben.'

He shakes Ben Ho's hand and gives him the card. 'I'll give this to you to hold on to for your sister. I have another party I have to go to now, but I'm glad to have met you both.'

He looks at me, lifts my hand in his, and does the bowing thing with his head again. 'It would be a shame for you to be hidden in a kitchen. I don't think the white apron suits you.'

He disappears.

Probably a hashish mirage.

I go into the bathroom. Very woody and captainical. I wash my hands, slide my finger into my throat, and throw up champagne and caviar. The caviar floats, and the membranes of the tiny eggs are still intact.

* * *

Ben Ho and I walk homewards through the narrow streets of the Marais. He's got a tape recorder and is recording the sounds – groups of people chattering in French, in Arabic, or in some French-African dialect; high heels knocking on the sidewalk, sirens, motorbikes. I stay quiet so I won't have to hear myself on the tape. I hate myself on tape. I sound different inside my head.

We pass by a tiny shop that sells nothing but absinthe, and he turns off the tape.

'I had fun tonight,' I say.

'Yeah? Are you gonna call that photographer?'

I can almost feel the photographer kissing my hand. The hairs stand up on my arm. 'I don't know. It's probably bullshit. I'm too fat to be a model.'

'You're not too fat. You're just fucked up. I don't think you see your body the way it really looks.'

'Thanks, I guess. I mean, would I rather be fucked up or fat? I think I'd rather be mildly fucked up.'

'I'm not so sure about the "mildly" part.' He turns his recorder back on and I whack him on the butt with my purse.

* * *

I dream that Mom is dead. She's lying on a blue-and-white-tile floor with her dark hair spilling off to one side in a tangled clump, and there are people all around, but no one else seems to see her, and I'm afraid that someone will step on her.

I try to get the attention of random passers-by. An old woman with blue hair smiles. Her teeth are sickeningly yellow. I try to stop her, but she doesn't see me, either.

All I can think to do is to kneel down by Mom, to

shield her. She doesn't have any make-up on. Her eyes and lips are pale. Mom always wears make-up, so I know she would be horrified. I brush her hair, but it starts to come out of her head as I brush. I take a tube of lipstick from my pocket. A bright red. My hands shake as I apply it to her lips, and I miss her mouth in places, so that it looks like the red pen circle that an impatient teacher might draw around a mistake. Her eyelids pop open, but her clear blue eyes don't register anything. They don't see me.

I slap her on the cheek, and when I wake up, my hand is shaking, and I still feel the slap.

It's dawn. I open my window and light a cigarette. Below me I watch a guy in a spring-green uniform sweep the sidewalk with a matching green broom. He's singing something to himself in a quavering voice, a voice from a place that hears a different scale, and as I listen to him and the rhythmic scratching of his broom, my hand stops shaking.

* * *

Had I not missed the class before and known what was coming, I definitely would have missed this day, too.

Chef Gaillard, after greeting me with a hostile glare, clenches a skinned rabbit. He's about to show us how to cut up a rabbit for stew.

He starts out by removing the liver. Which he saves. This alone is more than I can bear. I watch the Japanese guy in front of me take notes in carefully made letters.

Then Chef Gaillard trims off little flaps of skin and the tops of the forelegs of the hairless pink bunny. I don't know why I'm even watching. This cannot be good. He reaches for his cleaver. I focus in on the Japanese guy's notes again. I hear the whack! whack! and then a little diagram appears on the notebook, of three sections of rabbit.

The sound of breaking bones gets worse as the vivisection continues.

I find myself standing. Chef Gaillard pauses, blood-smeared cleaver in hand.

'I am not a chef,' I say.

He looks at me with every bit as much disgust as I feel for the rabbit pieces. 'C'est sur.'

I take off my white jacket, hang it on the back of my chair, and listen to the sound of my footsteps on the tile floor as I walk out of the kitchen.

When I get home, I hear Ben Ho in his bedroom with someone who giggles.

Yeah. Her. I recognize the irritating tone of her voice.

At least the Tempur-Pedic mattress doesn't make much noise. But I imagine it forming to the shape of her skinny little ass as it absorbs her heat, which is maybe even worse.

I picture her on Chef Gaillard's cutting board, and this image is comforting.

Remove liver; set aside. Trim off the extra flaps of skin, the bones of the forearm . . .

I go into the kitchen, pour myself the remains of a bottle of white wine from the refrigerator, locate my Vicodin in my purse, and swallow one of those for the sudden cramps that have attacked me. In the living room I sit down by the window and wait. In about twenty minutes the narcotic should tuck me into its soothing folds.

Unfortunately the clay army is stationed on this windowsill. They're all looking at me with their grim little faces.

Three cigarettes later the Vicodin and wine have done their thing. I'm perfectly calm when she emerges naked and sweaty-haired in the kitchen. She has a pleasantly nervous look on her face when she spots me.

'Hi,' I say. I light another cigarette and examine her exposed body. She's from California. She works with clay. She pretends not to be embarrassed about her nakedness.

'Hi there.' She actually walks up to me on her meatless legs. She has a round mole on her tiny left breast. 'Can I bum a cigarette?'

Sweet, sweet Vicodin. I take a gentle puff of my cigarette and watch the trail of smoke that slithers from the tip of it. In this light I notice that the smoke is actually made of two intertwining streams, one grey and one blue. I wonder if it's the ugly grey one that has all the stuff that's so bad for you. But maybe it's actually the pretty blue part that's lethal.

Ben Ho walks into the room wearing just his jeans. I follow the path of soft hair down into the valley of his stomach. He walks over to me and takes the cigarette from my hand, flicks the accumulated ashes into the ash-tray, and puts it back in my hand. His just-fucked hair hangs over his face, but he pulls it aside to look at me. His eyes bore through the Vicodin.

'Feel free to take a shower, Linda,' he says.

Her smell leaves the room. Without Ben Ho taking his eyes away from me.

His eyes are mine. They're mine.

* * *

When they leave I drop down on to my bed. I know how to make myself really, really small, even though I'm six feet tall. Tuck the head, tuck the knees. I like to stay very still. Hold myself and listen to my breath.

And today I let myself have my thumb.

* * *

When the ring of my cellphone wakes me up, it's dark outside. I must have slept for a long time. It's Ben Ho, asking me to meet him for dinner at a café on the rue de la Mairie.

I drink some water, smoke a cigarette, put on some shoes. There's a tremble in my legs that makes me feel wobbly. I drink some more water, take half a Xanax.

He's already at a table by the window when I get there. It's one of those classic Parisian places that have great sole meunière and life-beleaguered waiters who wear white shirts and black pants. There's a lot of slamming of plates on to tables.

'Hey.' Ben Ho pushes a glass of red wine my way.

'Hey.'

'So how come you weren't at your cooking school today?'

'How come you're hanging out with this Linda?' I say her name the way she would, in that annoying pseudo little-girl voice.

'Give her a chance. You've never liked any of my girl-friends.'

The waiter takes time out of his day to hand us our menus. I take a look at it. They serve rabbit here.

'I quit school today.'

'Shit, Meade. Why?'

'Chef Gaillard hates me. And he was demonstrating how to cut up a rabbit.'

'Oh.' He pours us each some more of the red. The ver-tical line of worry makes an appearance on his forehead. 'So what are you going to do? You want to stay in Paris, don't you? Just skip the rabbit and go back and learn how to make soups, or something.'

Our waiter reappears and is massively frustrated with us for not having made our ordering decisions yet. I know he'll punish us by waiting a long time to come back. I don't care. I'm not even hungry.

I'm going to get really thin. 'I think I'm going to call that photographer.' I can still almost feel the imprint of his lips on my hand.

'Ahhh.' His forehead a smooth sheet. 'Well, that's not a bad idea. You can probably get a visa that way. And it could be fun.'

I look down into the oily surface of my wine and see a red reflection of my eye. 'Did you hang on to his number?'

He pulls out his wallet and sorts through the various scraps of paper, foil, and chips of wood in there. 'I still have it.' He holds it where I can see it but not reach it. 'But if he says he wants to do pictures, I'm coming with you.'

The waiter reappears. 'Mademoiselle?' He hovers over me with his pencil poised on his pad of paper.

'Rien, merci.'

He actually says, 'Oh là là,' as he rolls his eyes upwards. I wonder what, if anything, exists for him beyond the tin ceiling, coated with years' worth of evaporated butter.

Ben Ho orders a bunch of things, including a sole meunière.

When the sole arrives, he feeds me little forkfuls now and then when I'm not thinking about it.

* * *

Sometimes my weirdnesses are very convenient. It's easy to lose weight, because my disgust for food intensifies so that I basically gag at the sight or smell of it most of the time.

In the evenings I go to a wine bar in the sixth that has the most soothing sandwich. Just a perfect baguette with a little butter and thin slices of a hard, nutty cheese. I can eat that.

After about a week and a half, my hip bones feel sharp enough for me to call him. Of course I take a Xanax first. I sit on a bench facing St Paul's Cathedral and watch the slow movement of the hands on the clock face until my blood feels like slush. Twenty-one minutes. Twelve o'clock.

My fingers only shake slightly as I dial his number.

'Allo?'

'Hi. Majid?'

'Yes. Who is this?'

'This is Meade. I met you at that party on the barge?'

'Ohhh, yes. The dancing twin. Who wants to be a chef.'

'Yeah. Well, not exactly. I've kind of given up on the chef idea.'

'A misfortune to the kitchens of the world, I'm sure.'

'I don't think so.' My heart, my blood and my mind

are all moving very slowly. The inside of my head feels like an echo chamber. An empty cathedral.

'And what can I do for you?' He says something in French to somebody else.

'Um, I was thinking about what you said. About modelling? Did you mean it? You said you could recommend an agent.'

'Of course.' I hear female laughter transmitting through his phone. 'Let me talk to a couple of people and get back to you. Can I reach you at this number?'

'Yeah.' I watch some birds flying around up by the church tower and wonder if they can feel the signal from the cellphone towers. 'Thanks, I appreciate it.'

'My pleasure.'

After we hang up I keep hearing the word 'pleasure'.

★ ★ ★

He actually meant it. I look in the mirror and wonder why. I'm in the bathroom, getting ready for my appointment with an agent, Marie-Hélène, and the *tarte aux légumes* that I had for lunch sits like an alien inside me, and I want to throw up, but Ben Ho is waiting for me, and I don't want him to hear the alien removal.

TARTE AUX LÉGUMES

eggs

cream

onion

zucchini

tomato

flour

butter

salt

herbes de Provence

I try to ignore the dense weight of the ingredients gestating in me, so I focus on lip-gloss application. This doesn't take long.

Of course I took my Adderall this morning, but would the heavy calm of Xanax be a good idea as a topper, so I don't get too nervous? Or maybe the mild euphoria of the Vicodin. I'm realizing that I can pretty much control the path of my moods, sensations and (preferably lack of) appetite with a carefully considered recipe of meds.

The goal is to achieve a state of . . . well, not nirvana, or anything, but upliftedness. To experience elevated moments. And if the downside is to feel rotten in the morning, I would rather have that than have to endure a flatlined existence. I think mornings can pretty much be written off, anyway. They're just a matter of controlled collateral damage. I prefer dusk to dawn.

I hear Ben Ho's impatient footsteps, and his rapid knock on the door. Tat tat tat tat tat tat tat. 'Come on, Meade. You're already beautiful. Let's go.'

I opt for a half of each. I quickly split the pills and swallow them, taking a big swig from the Vittel bottle because water's good for the skin.

* * *

By the time we get to the Métro I have a nice floaty feeling going. Colours look more saturated. The lavender of the Métro ticket is beautiful, sticking out like a little tongue from the slot at the gate entry.

Ben Ho throws his arm around me. I feel his tendons. But when he takes his arm away, and we sit down on the orange plastic seats of the train, I start to float out of my body. I hover near the ceiling and look down at my black boot crossed over my blue-jeaned knee. I watch Ben Ho's hand move as he sneakily sketches the people around him.

He pulls my hair and I drain back into my body, which

is a relief, because I have to get out and walk. We head through the tunnel of arches on the rue de Rivoli, past rows of silver Eiffel Towers arranged on shelves. When we get to the building I press an oversized doorbell and we're buzzed through the enormous door with its pretty gold and wrought-iron anti-thief bars.

When we step inside the giant birdcage of an elevator, Ben Ho starts whistling little tunes and tweets until I start laughing.

The elevator begins to rise, and it takes my stomach a moment to catch up. When the cage doors open, Ben Ho says, 'We're free!' and he pulls me out on to the landing. We're faced with a heavy metal door marked 'ICON!' I still feel like I'm going up in the elevator.

Ben Ho looks me in the eyes and pulls a strand of hair off my face. 'Ready, Mutchen?'

'Ready, Budelitz.'

We walk through the door together. Inside, good-looking people dressed in black stare into laptop screens and talk on headsets. The one stationed in front looks up and says, 'You must be Meade.' Which is totally weird, that she knows who I am. 'Marie-Hélène will be with you in a moment. Would you like a coffee?'

I calculate the possible effects of caffeine with my med cocktail and my levitating stomach. 'No, thanks.' My mouth is cottony and my tongue feels thick. 'Do you have some water?'

'Of course. A water for you. And you?' She tilts her head towards Ben Ho and smiles at him. She's dark-haired and petite. I think she's flirting with him.

'This is my brother, Ben,' I say, my mouth so dry that I can barely form the 'th' sound.

'Brother Ben, would you like a coffee or water?'

'I'm fine, thanks.'

She indicates chairs for us, but I only sit for a moment on the sleekly designed edge of it before she reappears with water and whisks me off to an inner office. I glance back at Ben Ho, but he's pulled out his sketchbook and isn't paying any attention to me.

A door is opened to a room not quite in proportion to the height of its ceiling. Tall potted palms flank a desk where a tiny woman with a beaky nose greets me with a thin-lipped smile. 'I'm Marie-Hélène.' She holds her hand out to me. It's cold, and the sharply cut diamonds on her ring scrape my fingers.

I guess we have a sort of conversation, the kind that

I'm forced to have at Mom and Dad's cocktail parties, but the words don't sink in, only the feeling of being examined by her appraising eyes. She asks me to walk, to turn around. I could be a filly on a lead rope being judged for confirmation. I half wonder if she's going to open my mouth to examine my teeth.

'Yes, you really are lovely,' she says.

On her desk are large prints of me, dancing on the barge. A row of pictures of models whose faces I've seen in magazines parades across her walls.

'Um, thank you.' I'm lovely? What does that mean?

She puts me through some more cocktail-party chatter. I guess she's just being polite. She probably doesn't like my thighs. I wonder if Ben Ho is chatting up the secretary. She might be more bearable than Linda.

And then she says, 'I think we will work very well together, no?' She opens a drawer and hands me a contract.

* * *

In the Métro on the way home, I show him my contract, and he shows me his drawing of the office filled with bird people up on swings, some of them pecking away at the keyboards on their suspended laptops.

'You should have seen Marie-Hélène. She totally looks like a bird.'

'Are you going to sign this?'

'I guess. Why not?'

'Maybe we should get a lawyer to look at it. But it looks pretty basic. They get fifteen per cent.'

'Okay. Well, right now I have nothing, so fifteen per cent of nothing is nothing.' Suddenly, I'm very queasy.

'So the idea is that they'll make it be fifteen per cent of something.'

'Something would be good.'

When we climb out of the Métro, I walk really fast to get home, as fast as Ben Ho walks on his own. I'm flying up the stairs, and when we're inside I put on music so he doesn't hear me throw up.

* * *

The signing of the contract also involves a swarm of black-clad employees measuring every inch of me. This is fairly humiliating, but less so than it might be because the numbers, which are in centimetres, mean nothing to me.

But they're all tiny women. I feel like Gulliver being enchained by these little people with their measuring

68

tapes. And they make comments to each other under their breath in rapid French that I can't understand. I'm almost sure I hear the word 'vache'.

They secretly think I'm a cow. They'll probably book me to appear in *Heifer* magazine. I keep hearing 'vache' as if it were being whispered into my ear on my way home.

Ben Ho cheers me up because he has champagne for me when I get back to the apartment, and that's great, champagne is great, but what's really fantastic is that when he opens the bottle, the cork launches across the room and annihilates two members of the clay army. They crash to the cobblestones below and die an unpleasant death. Ben Ho looks out the window and says, 'Shit!' but he doesn't go downstairs to retrieve their pulverized corpses.

This, I think, is an excellent omen.

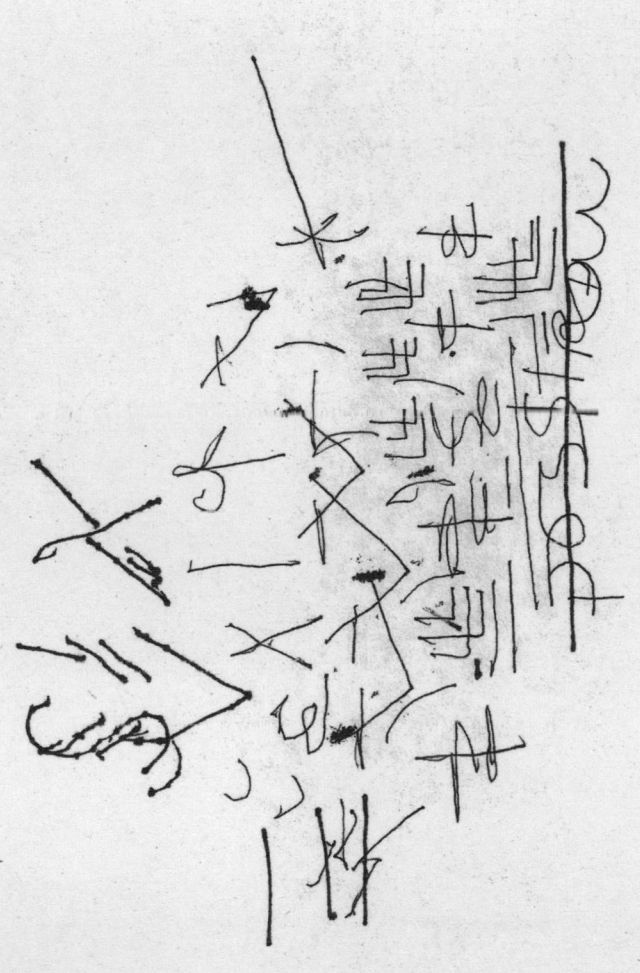

I hang out underneath the Moroccan tent that's set up in the corner of the studio and smoke while assistants and assistants to assistants set up lights in front of a crumbling brick wall. Unoccupied workers, Egyptian guys about my age whose jobs I have yet to figure out, play soccer on the other side of the vast space, using light stands as goal posts. One of them scores and jumps up, grabbing the rafter for a celebratory swing. I try not to be nervous, try not to even think about the fact that I'm about to be photographed for French *Vogue*, and the two Vicodins are helping, but they seem to have no control over sweat.

The make-up artist, a cheerful British woman of Jamaican descent, arranges her paint kit in front of a large mirror. Finally she calls me over to her station, so I stub out my cigarette and sit down on the rolling chair where I'm forced to stare at myself framed by light bulbs as she daubs at me. I watch my skin tone go blank as a canvas, my eyes enlarge, my cheeks blush, and my lips become the crimson focal point of my face.

I look like royal portraiture. It's me, sort of, but definitely a flattering version.

'Aren't we beautiful, love!' she says when she finishes her intricate labours, and she pinches my cheek before passing me off to the hairdresser.

The hairdresser's name is Radovan and he comes from Serbia, he says. He has a moustache and goatee and a black cross tattooed on his wrist. I shake his large-boned hand and then close my eyes for a moment, sitting very still as I concentrate on the stroke of his brush on my scalp, breathing in deeply as I continue to avoid thinking about *Vogue*.

When Majid emerges from his office, it's clear that he's master and commander. The CD volume decreases. The lighting guys make adjustments. The soccer players abandon their game and load film. Everyone in the room becomes perceptibly more focused and attentive.

I notice his relaxed and graceful stride as he approaches the hair station, where he looks not at me directly, but at my image in the mirror. Then he kisses my hand again, and my whole body sinks into a state of relaxation. I feel drugged. Very pleasantly drugged. Well, I am pleasantly drugged, but this is even better. His lips are almost purple. I have the urge to stick my fingers into his mouth.

'She needs some powder on the décolletage,' he says to Lily. 'Veronica! She's ready.'

Veronica, the stylist, stands next to a rack of clothes, scrutinizing me with a squint while Lily runs a sable brush over my chest and I try to will my sweat faucets into the OFF position. After I've been thoroughly dusted, I approach Veronica.

'Here. Put this on.' She has a deep voice and a deep tan and doesn't wear a scrap of make-up. She hands me a Dior men's suit. No shirt. Fears of underarm stains dance in my head.

I really like menswear, though. Once I'm suited up, I feel invincible.

Veronica runs her hands over the narrow jacket, testing the fit, and says, 'Purr-fect.' She adds a pearl-and-filigree necklace that reaches between my breasts.

The beautiful soft black leather men's shoes that she hands me are a struggle. 'They're too small,' I tell her.

'No problem. I'll cut off your toes.'

She looks like she would, too. I curl up my feet and

cram them into the shoes, which kind of crushes the invincibility vibe.

Majid reappears and examines me. 'Excellent.' He takes me by the hand and I hobble off with him over to the set. While we're walking, he runs his thumb once up the centre of my palm, which erases my feet from my mind.

He shows me the zone where I'm to stand. 'You get to be the male twin today,' he says, winking at me. 'You look fantastic. Fierce, but sensual.' He retreats to his camera and looks at me through the lens, and the way a lens can make a leaf go up in flames, it focuses energy on me, and something happens. It's not me any more. The camera sees me into beauty.

Majid is saying, 'Yes, baby, hold it. That's it. Beautiful. Yes!'

But the words don't matter much. The words and the clicking are a rap, a rhythm. The lens matters.

I go inside of it. I move through it. I come out the other side, somewhere else. Somewhere I've never been, into a sort of vortex that draws me and draws me. It shrinks me, it enlarges me.

It looks at me, at a part of me that I can't see.

Inside the body of the camera I'm alive. Tiny framed selves winding around a spool.

I'm made of light.

* * *

When the lens is through with me, I'm not sure what to do with myself. I'm wondering if Majid is going to ask me to go out with him afterwards or something, but he doesn't. Radovan is gone, Lily is gone, assistants scurry around packing clothes and putting things away. It's over. I'm wearing my regular jeans again, my sweater that has a small hole under the arm, and there's nothing to do but leave.

'Bye, Majid,' I say.

'You were great. I knew you would be. I'm sure we'll see one another soon.' This time, when he kisses my hand, he looks me in the eyes so intensely that I feel like we're having sex, only it's a lot less messy.

* * *

I'm craving a cigarette, and a drink would be nice, too. When I walk through the door of our apartment, Ben Ho lunges at me, flips me around, and pins me to the

ground. The former high-school State Champion wrestler holds me down so that I can't move at all. He knows
when to let me go before I freak out, though.

He eases up on me, so that I feel the light, steady pressure of his weight on my legs and stomach, which I don't
try to resist. A hunk of his hair hangs over my face, and I
breathe in the sweet, oily smell of it, this oil that's like an
energy source for me, igniting cellular activity throughout my body.

'You're a terrible wrestler,' he says. 'You don't even
try.'

'Well, I guess I'll drop all my dreams of joining the
World Wrestling Federation, then.'

'How was your day of being groomed, pampered and
admired?'

'Weird.'

'Good weird, or bad weird?'

'Both. I was really nervous at first.'

'I know. I could feel it from here. I started sweating.'

'You did?' I love when I penetrate his calmness, when
he feels my feelings.

'Yeah. But then it got better. Around three o'clock.'
He shifts his weight on to his heels.

'That was probably when I actually got in front of the camera. There's something about looking into the lens . . .'

'You liked that, huh?'

'Yeah.'

He leans down so close to me that our eyelashes are almost touching. 'You liked it a lot.' He sits up again, still looking at me. 'Nice face paint.'

'Thanks. Hey, what do we have here to drink?'

'Le whisky. You want one?'

'Definitely.'

'Good. Then you can go get it. Would you get me one, too?' Ben Ho rolls off of me into a backwards somersault before springing to his feet.

I hum quietly, tunelessly to myself as I fill two glasses in the kitchen and bring them back into the living room. We sit down, sip our drinks and light each other's cigarettes.

I take a very satisfying drag and blow a perfect smoke ring that encircles his nose. 'Seriously. I think I could be pretty good at this.'

'Yeah? Well, just don't start carrying around a small creature purporting to be a dog and dating a guy named Mario. Or Majid. Promise?'

'Promise. Mostly.'

He abandons me on the couch, and I sink back into the down cushions with my whisky. I know I'm not going to get any more conversation out of him while he tornadoes around the room.

It would be especially hard to talk, anyway, because he puts his 1930s English-language-learning record on the turntable, which just throws out random phrases. I don't think you could ever actually learn English from it.

Please part my hair on the side.

Ben Ho gathers his telephones. There are seven of them, and they're all red.

I would prefer for you to use hair tonic, but no oil.

He has a drill in his hand. He attacks the wall.

My gloves are in the drawer.

Soon he's hammering, and I can feel it inside my skull.

Please prepare a gin and tonic for me.

He's mounting the telephones on the wall. They're tabletop models, so the effect is disorienting. Also he's pulled all of the receivers off their bases, and stretched their curly cords so that it looks as if the receivers are climbing towards the ceiling, some of them crossing over each other on their way up.

I will require temporary lodging.

I finish my whisky. 'Hello, hello? Calling Ben Ho.' But I know he won't answer.

* * *

It's very easy to throw up the whisky, which is good, because it's fat-making stuff. I don't even have to use my finger. I just open myself to the idea of emptying, kneel down by the toilet, and it's gone. I flush the toilet at the same time to hide the sound. It's very quick.

When I rinse out my mouth I accidentally glance at myself in the mirror, but this time I can't look away. I stare at this person in the mirror and try to feel a sense that it's me, but I just don't feel it. Lily's make-up is a bit startling when examined close up – I can see the flesh-toned layer of powdered foundation that is pretending to be skin, and the inky lines around my eyes, the mascara coating my blonde lashes – but the person in the mirror isn't a stranger because of the make-up. I touch my mouth and watch the mirror-person touch her mouth, and for some reason this makes me start to cry.

When I see the crying person who has trembling lips, red eyes and black tears, this person who's working to suck in a little air, I begin to calm down. This, this is me.

I take a Xanax and go to bed.

* * *

Days melt into one another, days of walking around the city alone, riding the Métro alone. Sometimes I see other models, a clearly recognizable breed of gangly, underground creatures with portfolios propped between their knees. I go from appointment to appointment, popping out of the Métro *sortie* and finding myself in a different neighbourhood, with no sense of what connects it to the last neighbourhood, besides the metal tracks.

Today I saw a rat on the tracks.

Today I have my period and the blood is flowing so heavily that I feel like a victim of war.

I walk into a studio and meet a German photographer named Max. He's scruffy and old and he murmurs incomprehensibly while he looks at my portfolio of pictures.

Rats and blood. Rats and blood.

'Where are you from?' he asks me. His eyes are the colour of a grimy nickel.

'Nashville.'

'Ah. The city of Elvis.'

'Yeah. Elvis.' I don't bother to explain that Elvis was from Memphis, that he only recorded in Nashville.

'Come, Miss Presley. Let me take a couple of Polaroids.'

I stand in front of seamless white paper and look into his lens.

I like Polaroids. I like the sound of them being spit out of the camera, and I like to watch the blank paper with its swirl of chemicals slowly form a ghostly image of me. I wish you could make them stop at this point, before they develop further and become too clear, too sharp.

But Max seems pleased. He touches my hair. 'The colour is real?'

'It's real.'

'Beautiful.'

'Thanks.' I rest one hand on my hip and register with deep pleasure that I can feel the underneath side of the bone.

When I get back to the apartment, the sky is a dull grey and my feet hurt. Ben Ho's not home. I call him and he doesn't answer. I hate being alone. Vicodin and a bath. I stretch out in water so hot that it makes my skin pinken, and wait for the pain to go away.

I dial Ben Ho from the bathtub. I focus my twin powers on him, picturing him answering the phone. He's in his black sweater, there are tiny beads of sweat on his upper lip, he has a paintbrush in his hand. 'Answer!' I even say it out loud.

He still doesn't answer.

A layer of city grime, sweat and strangers' breath sits on the tension of the water's surface. I sweep it all towards the overflow drain.

Take a deep breath and dial again. Smoke a cigarette using a soap dish as an ashtray and dial again. Brush my hair and put on lipstick and dial again. Swig of whisky and dial again.

I scream at my phone and snap it shut. I want to smash it to little toxic pieces on the floor, but Ben Ho might call, so I take another swig of whisky and head to the studio.

★ ★ ★

I go straight to the painting studio. He's there. Wearing his black sweater. Linda is definitely in the room, lying on a draped platform. Naked. I see the now familiar arrangement of bones, the mole on her breast.

'What are you doing here?' is how he greets me.

I shrug. 'Just thought you might be here.'

At least they're not alone. There are several others hovering over blobs of colour, squinting at canvases, making comments in French or English or some language that's completely unrecognizable to me. Maybe they're speaking in tongues.

Ben Ho keeps painting. He doesn't look at me. He doesn't look at me, he stares at her body or the tip of his brush.

'Hi, Meade,' says Linda in her squeaky-toy voice.

'You can pour us all some whiskies, if you want,' he says. He gives me a flicker of eye, then looks towards the whisky. Back to Linda. 'I'm going to take a break in a minute.'

I glance over his shoulder as I walk whiskywards, and I'm somewhat relieved to see that his painting of her looks more medical than erotic. He hasn't painted the drapey fabric. She seems to be lying on a gurney, and her skinny body is grotesque.

I pour the whiskies. He sets down his brush and lights a cigarette.

'Can I move now?' I think she says.

'Sure. Just try to remember your pose.'

Fortunately it's chilly in the studio, and she wraps herself in a long sweater, so I don't have to look at her nipples.

He looks at me now, carefully, steadily.

'Remember, Ben Ho? How we used to paint each other's bodies with our finger-paints?'

A giggle from over there somewhere.

'I don't know if I actually remember, or if I remember from Mom's pictures.' He downs his whisky.

'I remember. I painted around your diaper. And I remember using all these bright colours – blue and yellow, green and red – and I was so disappointed when I'd finished because you just looked like you were covered in mud.'

'You can't possibly remember.' That voice. 'From when you were in diapers? I don't think so.'

We both ignore her. Ben Ho dips his finger in paint and draws a line gently down my nose.

★　★　★

After a few more whiskies I lie down on a tarp in the corner. Voices in the room sound echoey and weird. I start hearing them as tones rather than words, swelling and quieting. I touch the now dry paint streak on my nose and it feels comforting.

I remember the pictures, too. Ben Ho and I with our little painted bodies, squinting in the sunlight on our back deck. Mom liked to take pictures of us. She'd amass them over the year for the sole purpose of choosing the best one for her Christmas card. She framed us carefully. She shut the eye that wasn't engaged with the viewfinder. Her concentration was completely on us.

Not like when I talked to her. I'd tell her about the boy next to me at school who picked his nose and wiped his finger inside his desk, carefully holding the desktop an inconspicuous inch open. My nightmare visions of the inside of his desk. Or I'd describe in great detail the plot of some book I was reading, but after I'd been talking for an embarrassingly long time, I'd realize that my mother wasn't listening. I could see it in her filmy eyes.

In her mind, she didn't live in our kitchen, in our den. Maybe she built another house in her head, maybe she was here in Paris; maybe she was in her childhood home in Atlanta, a home that like large chunks of Atlanta doesn't exist any more. Maybe she was window-shopping on Fifth Avenue in New York, maybe she was fucking a stranger. I don't know.

I close my eyes and gently breathe in paint dust, tiny particles that colour the inside of my lungs. Beautiful, beautiful, bright pixels.

* * *

It's a chilly evening and Ben Ho and I have a fire going, we're drinking red wine, and I'm feeling euphoric, little waves of a contentment that includes excitement, sweet flutters on all my nerve endings, as if they're blooming into small, white, very fragrant flowers. This is almost the last of my Vicodin supply, which Mom gave me.

She had loads after her last little surgical procedure (eyes), and she's pretty generous with the elevating pills.

I'm not too worried about running out, because you can get codeine at the pharmacies here, which should be an acceptable substitute.

We stare into the fire and watch the tender licks of flames on logs.

But Ben Ho can never stay still for very long. He bolts from the fireplace and reappears from his room wheeling a stroller. A vintage stroller, with a blue velvet exterior, cream-coloured patent-leather interior, and rubber-and-chrome wheels.

'What do you think?' He's got a proud-father glow.

'Are you expecting?'

'Yeah, right.' He adjusts the angle of the back of the seat. 'I needed something with wheels.'

'Those are stylish wheels.'

'Pour us a couple more glasses of wine and then we'll go for a walk.'

I refill our glasses, but he only takes a sip, so I end up drinking both mine and his while he lopes around the apartment, gathering stuff. He uses clamps to mount four cameras on monopods on the stroller, quickly setting each one up with a different height and angle. Then he spends a long time programming four remote controls, which he attaches to the handle.

'Any desire to tell me what you're doing?'

'Oh, just taking some random pictures.'

I help him carry the stroller down the stairs, and then Ben Ho is pushing the stroller beside me, and it's night time, so he's got the flashes triggered, too, and the flashes go off in some alternating, intermittent pattern. I don't know what the cameras are seeing, briefly illuminated pieces of buildings, pieces of people, pieces of pavement, of sky, I guess, but I see a lot of puzzled faces, and I see Ben Ho next to me, smiling.

★ ★ ★

I dream that I'm sitting in a corner of my bedroom in Mom and Dad's house playing, but I'm just a head, and the game is to sort through the big pile of body parts in front of me and put them together. I find an arm and begin to rummage around. Here's a foot, there's a section of stomach, but I can't manage to put them together in the right order. Also there seem to be some pieces missing.

I wake up because I have to pee, but it takes me a long

time to get out of bed. I lie with my eyes closed, feeling the subtle peaks and valleys that my body forms in the mattress, and wishing that I had a bedpan.

I think I prefer being asleep to being awake.

* * *

Outside my window a thick grey sky sags over the city. I move my body from the bed one section at a time and watch the mattress's indentations swell back up, as if I had never been there.

Ben Ho is gone. His breakfast remnants rot in the kitchen sink. The thick air from outside has snuck in through the cracks beneath the windows and grips my head.

Adderall and coffee don't work today. I can't bring myself to get dressed, much less walk out the door into the flow of people who just seem like projections, like I'm trying to act in front of a screen of images that are flat and fake. I can't pretend any more.

I call my booker, Françoise. This is a woman who sits on a chair on wheels and talks on the phone all day, a commodity broker of sorts, and I am one of her commodities. She has a cheerful, round face and messy black hair. I tell her I'm sick. I tell her to cancel my appointments. She makes little sounds of concern in a French accent.

I get one of Ben Ho's dirty shirts from his room, a very soft navy blue shirt that I hold next to my face. I rub the edges of it with my fingers and breathe in his scent, the sweet oil of his hair, the toasted tobacco, and that indescribable note that I feel travel up and down my spine that is his essence.

* * *

A double dose of Adderall and more coffee starts to work and suddenly I am *pleine d'énergie* and so I go outside and I start walking, very, very fast. I pass a lot of people. They're just a blur of trench coat or red scarf or dark glasses or shopping bags or jutting baguettes. Cobblestones, dusty shop windows, wooden signs with peeling letters, a withered French flag. I get to the river and it's in a big rush, too, rushing gloomily along, grey-greenly along, within its bricked banks, its bridges, and I wonder if it feels confined. But rivers can't really be confined, that's the beautiful thing about rivers, the sly power of water, carving through rock or whatever gets in its way. My feet tap tap tap across the wooden bridge, and then I slip into a random café and stand at the bar for a shot of espresso and a cigarette, the Paris speedball, along with several other rush-cravers. Coffee in the right hand, cigarette in the left. I notice that my hands are almost trembling, as if they have a mild electric current running through them.

The man next to me, tall, in a black coat, with a wave of silver hair rolling across his head, starts looking at me in that way, like he might say something. I stare intently at my hands and zoom inwards. And then I can't escape from a gruesome image: my hand, rolled in breadcrumbs, frying in a cast-iron pan.

The man doesn't talk to me. I stub out my cig, plunk my euros down on the counter and head back out, but I don't know where I'm going exactly, and I want to stop thinking about the fried hand, and I feel so weird and I don't want to be alone any more, I want to be with Ben Ho, at home with Ben Ho, and really, for her sake, it'd be better if Linda's not there, but I think she is, I think she is. She's infiltrating.

* * *

As I climb the stairs to our apartment, I imagine an army of twins marching behind me, two by two, with linked arms, holding pickaxes. Twenty sets of male/female twins. They're silent except for their heavy footsteps.

I open the door and proceed into the kitchen. She's there, leaning against the kitchen counter eating an apple: the temptation, the traitor. Ben Ho is slicing cheese.

'Hey,' he says without even looking up at me. She says nothing with her mouthful of forbidden fruit, but continues gnashing her teeth.

It's amazing how well my fist fits into her eye socket, as if it were designed to be there: my fist, her hollow. When I recoil my arm, readying myself for one more insertion, I see the rabbit fear appear in her, and she ducks her head, shields her eyes with her hands. The cheese knife clatters to the floor, and my army drops their pickaxes; and then with a few twists from Ben Ho, I am pinned on the ground, unable to move, his knee across my chest. My heartbeat thumps into his leg. I relax into him, allowing his weight on me, absorbing it. His hair hangs down over his face, and I don't even have to touch it to feel its smoothness interrupted by tangled sections.

'What the fuck are you doing?' His breath charges and retreats, out of his mouth, into his mouth. I watch his face as he yells at me – 'ruining my life!' – but I stop hearing his words as he takes one hand to my neck and begins to squeeze, constricting my airway. My body quakes as a deeply implanted thrill rises up my spine.

Her wailing is a distant siren, the comforting sound of a patrolled city.

A dark city, a night-time city, with cosy lights burning in windows, making me so sleepy. Overcome by the sweet narcotic of sleep.

* * *

Shattering glass wakes me up (a riot in the city? a brick thrown through a storefront window?) and it takes me a moment to realize that I'm in his bed. I immediately sense the Lindalessness in the apartment.

I watch him have a temper tantrum. It's the same as it's always been as long as I can remember. Basically he throws things around the room. Pencils roll, a coffee mug shatters against the radiator, books, shoes, bedding and a miner's lantern all hit the floor. Then he kicks a metal trashcan until it's reshaped. This seems to be the grand finale.

'Sorry,' I say, but I don't even convince myself. There was something scarily elating about punching her – the pure, adrenal high, but most of all, the deep satisfaction of the moment of contact, just like when you swing a baseball bat and hit the pitched ball, the sound of it hitting the wood, the feeling of impact travelling down the bat and into your hands.

He sits on the bed and smokes a cigarette, using a piece of the mug as an ashtray. Then he riffles through the bathroom and comes back with a tube of arnica gel, which he silently applies to my bruises, purple replicas of his fingertips.

The make-up artist, this one an Italian wearing pink corduroy pants and a gold Roman warrior-style medallion
on his free-weight-fortified chest, gasps when I sit down
in front of the mirror.

'My God! What happened to you?'

'I don't want to talk about it. It was very traumatic.'

'My poor beauty. We will make it disappear.' He turns
to his bottles of flesh-coloured liquid.

He paints my neck, my face, and even my breasts. I'm
to be emerging from a giant pink rose, as if shot out of a
flower cannon. Or maybe I'm a stamen. He takes a make-
up sponge to my nipples, tinting them a rosier hue. It
feels really weird to have a guy in pink pants breathing
his peppermint breath on me and dabbing at my nipples
while murmuring, 'Bella.'

When I'm standing in front of Majid's camera, I can't
help it. My nipples get erect.

He, however, isn't looking at my nipples. He's staring at my neck. For a long moment, he doesn't move. He doesn't say anything.

And then he approaches me.

'Let me get some powder,' says Pink Pants nervously.

Majid takes a chunk of my hair softly into his hands, winds it around my neck and resumes his position behind the lens, as if in a trance.

* * *

This time he asks me to dinner afterwards. I stare at the menu, trying to find something that I feel okay letting inside of me, something green, maybe. A salad with slices of pear in it. I'm not sure about the Roquefort cheese with its little blue veins, like in my grandmother's hands. I could either just avoid the Roquefort, or I could ask for the salad without it, but risk the withering look of the sleekly groomed waiter, and what if Majid would think that's weird, too? I better just brush the cheese chunks carefully aside with the tines of my fork.

I set the menu down and am aware that Majid has been watching me, not his own menu. I pull out a cigarette.

My heart is rattling the bars of my ribcage, which is making my hands shake a bit, too. I will them into steadiness. Majid lights a match for me, and I bring my tip to his flame.

'Thank you.'

Majid lights one himself. He keeps staring at me. My neck itches under my turtleneck collar. 'You're a very dark person, aren't you?' he finally says.

'I don't know. I think basically the whole world is suffering from one giant panic attack, don't you? People just deal with it in different ways.'

'So how do you treat this attack?'

'Drugs help.'

He laughs. His ash is accumulating, and I have the urge to flick it. 'And where does this darkness, this panic, come from for you?'

Two inches of ash, just in time, drop into the ashtray. I shrug.

He sucks on his cigarette some more. 'Well, it adds to your beauty, you know. To be so golden and light of hair and skin, but to have such a brooding quality in your eyes. That's why I love to photograph you.'

When I focus in on his eyes, everything else swirls into oblivion. There's something unnerving about them.

'You don't exactly seem like Mr Sunshine, yourself. Or a fashion guy. How'd you end up being a fashion photographer?'

'I suppose it was a rebellion of sorts.'

'Rebellion against what?'

He stubs out his cigarette and leans back in his chair. 'Well, in my country –' I'm wondering what his country is, but I don't want to interrupt, '– I was arrested for taking pictures.'

'What were you taking pictures of?'

'Someone being arrested.' He smiles and traces one finger along my cheekbone. 'Anyway, when I left Iran, I wanted to make photos again, and because there, women are forced to cover themselves with the chador, to hide themselves, their beauty, I wanted to reveal beauty. Expose it.'

There's something irresistible happening. I can feel the electrical field pulsating all around his body. I move through it to touch his hand. 'When you look at me, I feel very exposed.'

'You are,' he says.

There's a voltage surge inside of me. It's very hard to eat when the food arrives.

* * *

As he walks me back to the Marais, we pass underneath a window and hear someone playing the cello, then stop, and lean against the corner of a building worn smooth by years of wind and rain and other people leaning, other people pressed up against its surface, kissing.

Our tongues are committed to each other. They're like two small animals that stroke each other, roll over one another. He holds the back of my head firmly as he presses his mouth against mine. Occasionally we pause for breath. He slips his thumb down into my turtleneck and gently presses on my windpipe, and our tongue-animals become ferocious, and the building holds me up.

We kiss our way over the river and through the city, walking, kissing, walking, kissing, until we get to the doorway to my building. I open the outer door, and then we kiss in the dark, narrow hallway that leads to the courtyard and the stairs. There's a damp, stony smell.

'Do you want to come up with me? Say hi to Ben?'

He touches each of my nipples so lightly through my sweater and says, 'I want to stay hungry for a while.' He presses against me, and I wonder if his come has a mineral taste, and he says, 'I don't want to talk to your brother right now.'

'My twin.'

'Your twin.'

'Okay.' I take a couple of his fingers into my mouth for a moment, and then I let him suck my thumb.

Until I hear the unmistakable sound of Ben Ho bolting down the stairs, two steps at a time, accompanied by the rattling of glass, and I wonder if he felt me down here, finger to mouth with Majid, to choose this moment to bring down the recycling. We're right next to the recycling bin.

I pull out my thumb before he rounds the corner.

'Hi, Ben Ho. Do you remember Majid?'

Ben Ho smiles with only one side of his mouth as he shakes Majid's hand. 'Hey.'

'How are you?'

'Fine. You?' But any response that Majid might offer is drowned out by Ben Ho methodically dropping wine bottles into the bin, one by one, with enough force to clank loudly, but not enough to break glass.

* * *

I can still taste Majid's thumb, the woody notes of it, until I drink the wine that Ben Ho sets down in front of me. He sits across from me and says, 'Let's make another empty.'

He never slurs, he never stumbles, but his eyes are raging drunk, boring through my head and focused on a point two feet behind me, as if I'm invisible.

* * *

Two Xanax tonight: one for Majid, to quiet my craving for his searching tongue, and one for Ben Ho.

Please please please, God, make him reconnect. I have to have his eyes, his eyes, my lifeline, umbilical cord, we shared a womb, were embryos together, little embryos, weird translucent heads with giant eyes, curled bodies-to-be, growing fingers, growing toes, only twins know what it's like to go back that far together, back to that dark place, and it's peaceful in there, and it goes whoosh! whoosh! whoosh! beautiful pumping rhythm, never stops.

Two Xanax spread their little numbing tentacles through my brain until it's quiet in there, like being buried under snow, and there's nothing to do but sleep.

* * *

I don't know which pill to take today.

The door to Ben Ho's room is closed. He usually leaves it open. I press my ear against it, I listen for a long time until I think I hear the molecules of wood bumping into each other in some crazy, wood-defining pattern. So I open it. Ben Ho is sleeping.

I tiptoe closer to him. The covers are only pulled up to his waist, and his pale chest is bare. I want to touch his smooth skin. His dark pile of hair covers his whole face so that I worry that he might suffocate, but of course I see the calm rise and fall of his chest. Still, I carefully comb his hair off of his face with my fingers, and he opens his eyes.

He's not conscious enough to be mad, so he looks at me simply, from the distance of his dreams, but he's looking at me and I feel the flicker of connection. He even gives me a sleepy smile.

I kiss his forehead, right on his chicken-pox scar, and

he closes his eyes again, and I travel with him into his dream.

On the horizon, trees in flame. A field of animals: tigers, dogs, kangaroos, rabbits, running, not in a panic, but as if they're expertly participating in a marathon race.

* * *

Françoise, my booker at Icon!, calls me:

'Another booking with *Vogue* for you, chérie. The pay is not so great, but the exposure will be fantastic. This is a shoot in Russia, in St Petersburg, so we'll have to work on your visa.'

'Who's the photographer?'

'Majid. He adores you.'

A shivery wave moves through my body, and I don't think it's the Adderall.

The first thing I notice when we arrive at the St Petersburg airport is the bad, yellow, unsteady fluorescent lighting that makes everyone look like cadavers, even the two beautiful Russian models. Actually, especially them, because they are so skinny that it's hard to believe they're able to get around on those spindly legs. I look really fat next to them.

We all stand and stare at the slow revolutions of the luggage conveyor. The same three bags keep going around. I feel groggy from the Xanax I took so that I wouldn't get claustrophobic on the plane. I wish Ben Ho were here.

I pull my cellphone out of my pocket and press the ON button to see if it works here, so I can call him, but then a uniformed dude grabs my phone from my hands and says, 'Nyet!' along with some other things. Of course I have no idea what he's saying, but he seems really mad.

One of the Russian models, Nastia, comes up to me and says, 'You cannot use phone here.' She says a few things to the dude, which seem to convince him to give me my cell-phone back. He keeps yelling at me, though, and pointing to a sign I can't read. I lower my head in penitence for attempted phone usage and put it back in my pocket.

When I look at Majid I see sweat rolling down his face. 'What's the matter?' I ask him, and I touch his forearm. He doesn't exactly shake me off, but it's almost like he's fighting himself not to.

'Nothing. I'm fine.'

'Okay,' I say, but I step back from him, and try not to cry.

In the taxi to the hotel he sits up front, with the driver. I'm squeezed into the backseat next to Nastia, thigh to thigh. Her thighs are just the way I want mine to be. Nothing squishy about them. They're as hard as Ben Ho's.

And when I think of him my stomach aches. I look out the window and try to transmit everything I see to him: the cracked windshield of the taxi, the oily grey curls of the driver's hair spilling over his collar, the huge scale of the avenue leading into the city.

Nastia and Olya speak softly to each other in Russian. The sounds all seem generated from their noses and throats. We come to a red light, and a military monster truck pulls up next to us. The top of the truck's wheel is level with the roofline of the taxi. I peer up to see what the soldiers inside look like.

Nastia jabs me with her elbow. 'Don't look at them. They don't like when you look.'

'I thought Russia was supposed to be free now.'

'Free, yes. But soldier is still soldier.'

Majid is not looking.

* * *

The hotel bathroom is clean, with a hand-held shower which I use to hose off travel grime and clinging germs. Then I brush my teeth. Bacteria are little animals. They pee in your mouth. They eat the gunk in between your teeth. My room is a garret, with door windows leading out on to the silver rooftop, and another window that's like a porthole. I look out at the surrounding rooftops, watch them bounce the sunlight off of themselves, throwing colours into the pitch.

There is a knock on my door, which is equipped with a peephole. Through its convex lens I see a small, bulging image of Majid. When I open the door, it all happens very fast. He's lifting me, his foot shuts the door behind him, I'm flat on my back on the bed, covered by his pressing body, my clean mouth filled with his tongue. And then just as suddenly he's on his feet, moving back towards the door. He says, 'You need to be in the lobby in fifteen minutes.'

* * *

I stand between the lens and the Church of Our Saviour on Spilled Blood. I love that name. But the Spilled Blood isn't grim at all. The multicoloured onion domes look like party hats. And I'm dressed for a party, in a long, filmy sheath of red fabric. Nastia and Olya are looking very military. Olive drab wool. Square shoulders and lots of buttons. They're nice and warm. I'm freezing. They're on either side of me. Soldiers. Soldiers being watched by more soldiers. In the distance, they're there, watching us.

'They're coming to get you, Meade. Resist! Resist! Act like you're about to strike Nastia.'

I swing my bare arm, my clenched fist.

'Beautiful.'

If only Nastia were Linda! I could insert my fist into her other hollow.

Olya grabs me around the waist, stopping my motion.

'Great, Olya. Perfect. Swing again, Meade.'

Behind Majid, the soldiers move closer.

'Nastia! Olya! Grab her! Each take an arm!'

At first it's okay, but after a while of not being able to move my arms, panic blooms inside of me. This is the point when Ben Ho would know to let me go. Ben Ho, be with me now. Let me go.

The soldiers approach, moving as one. Trained twins, with their matching shorn heads and uniforms. Majid stops shooting. Nastia and Olya drop their hold on my arms. The producer of the shoot, a velvet-voiced Brit named Michael, puts himself between Majid and the soldiers.

'Can I help you?' he asks. His translator, a small, wiry guy with wire-rimmed glasses, echoes him in Russian.

The soldiers demand permits for the shoot. Michael hands them papers, which they scrutinize with mutual frowns. I glance at Majid and see a muscle twitch in his jaw.

The soldiers take their time, passing the paperwork back and forth to each other, examining it carefully. Then they ask for everybody's passports and visas, and they read through these as if they were poems. Everyone on set is quiet.

Then something that the translator says seems to break the spell, and they abruptly hand all the papers and passports back to Michael. They walk off along the canal, their steps synchronized. One of them emits a short bark of laughter. The other takes one last look at us over his shoulder, and then they turn off on to a side street.

As soon as they're gone, Majid grabs me rather roughly and pulls me back towards the church.

'Nastia and Olya, grab her again. Come on. We're losing light. I want you to go completely limp, Meade. Let them carry your weight.'

He gets behind his camera again. 'Drag her towards me!'

I hang between them, all resistance gone.

* * *

Later I find myself suspended by wires from an eighty-foot-high ceiling, wearing a designer spacesuit: silver spandex with a triangular neoprene inset for the torso, and three neoprene bands circling my legs. Radovan gave me an anti-gravity hairstyle that looks like three blonde pyramids pointing up from my head. I'm the lost cosmonaut, in eternal oblivion. A very good role for me. Below me, on the unforgiving marble floor of the State Museum, are three Russian artists, barefooted and dressed in rough tunics, playing electronically distorted folk instruments. The sound bounces madly against the marble surfaces, and when the lights are lowered and a spotlight is trained on me, another on the musicians, I can't see anything, and it's only through the acoustics that I can feel the immensity and near emptiness of the room, and I feel the adrenalized thrill of floating in space.

Which are my instructions, coming from a tiny earphone inside my right ear, Majid's voice, 'Float.'

So I stretch out, silver-suited, in the light-strobing air.

★ ★ ★

I'm to meet him in his room for dinner. A whispered command, a whispered number. 'I'm going to feed you,' he says.

In my room, before I go to him, I try to call Ben Ho. My cellphone doesn't work here, which makes me really anxious. A team of miniature gymnasts are doing a tumbling routine inside my stomach. I fumble in the night-table drawer, looking for telephone instructions and wondering if there will be a Bible in there, too, like in American hotels. Instead there is a supply of condoms.

I feel so empty without Ben Ho. I want Majid inside

me. Something to fill me up. Not just the tongue, I need him in the centre of my being, to knock the fucking gymnasts out of me and remove this hollow ache. I put three condoms in my pocket.

No telephone instructions. I call the hotel operator and feel breathlessly dependent on him to connect the wires, to connect me to Ben Ho.

And the gymnasts perform soaring leaps as the telephone is ringing in Paris. One ring. Two rings. Three rings. Fuck. Four rings. Ben Ho's recorded noises. Not even his voice.

* * *

Perfume, lip gloss and Xanax. Deep breath. Glass of water. Two cigarettes. Brush teeth. Check body in mirror for fat places. Get ready to face the enemy: food.

And he means it literally, he's going to feed me. In his room is a room-service table, its white-clothed surface laden with blinis, chopped egg, sour cream, onions, caviar. And vodka.

He rolls all the ingredients up in a blini and holds it to my lips. I can't do it. Not the sour cream, not the eggs.

'Eat.'

The edge of the blini is touching my lips. His eyes are also on my mouth. I take a tiny, tiny bite from the edge that doesn't have all the stuff in it. To my relief, he sets it back down on the plate and pours vodka into small stemmed glasses.

'In Russia you have to drink it in one shot. It's bad luck to set the glass back down unless it's empty,' he tells me. 'To you!'

'To you.' I swallow. The vodka rolls down in a clear, smooth path through all the tunnels inside me.

Then he picks up a silver spoon, scoops up just caviar with it, and holds that to my mouth. I'm finding myself in an obedient trance and open my lips to the clustered black balls of glistening caviar.

After another shot of vodka, I feel calm and lucid. When we kiss, our mouths taste spotlessly clean. My limbs go slack. He's lifting me, placing me on the bed. We taste each other's mouths again and I think that I may in fact die if I don't feel him inside me.

* * *

A perfectly formed, splashless dive into sleep. Quiet, dark, deep. But sometime in the deep night, I come shooting back up to the surface propelled by his screams. The tone and timbre of them petrify me, and even more so when I look at his face and see that he's asleep, that the screaming emanates from a place that I can't see. I want to make it stop, wake him up, but I'm scared to do that, too. Who will he be, what will he see, when he wakes up? I feel my heartbeat in my throat.

I touch his arm softly and he jerks upright, his eyes popping open terror-filled, a terror that communicates itself to me so completely that I feel it too, pure animal fear. And I smell it, reeking from his pores.

'Majid?' I touch his shoulder this time, and after a moment he sees me and we wrap ourselves around each other and let the terror wash over us. He exhales a lungful of air.

'What were you dreaming?'

He lets go of me. 'I'm going to pour a drink. You want one?'

'Definitely.'

We drink. He lights a cigarette.

'You really fucking scared me. What was it?'

His face is in profile to me, and I study the elegant lines of his long nose. He looks sideways and down at me.

'I spent some years as a political prisoner in Iran. When I was very young. Seventeen. Sometimes I have nightmares about it.' He brings his cigarette back to his mouth.

It takes a moment before these words even make sense to me, and then I know that I'm looking at a man to whom horrible things have happened.

'What . . . what happened to you there?'

He pours another drink and throws it down the back of his throat. Then he starts laughing, but it's a weird kind of laughter that makes my arm hairs stand at attention. 'The university! That's what we used to call it. Some of us spent our university years there.'

'Jeez,' I say. I feel really stupid, but this is so unfathomable to me that I don't know what else to say.

He doesn't seem to want to reminisce any further. After a few more shots of vodka, we go back to bed, and I'm lying on his warm chest, listening to his metronome heart, but for a long time after he's asleep, I can't even bring myself to close my eyes, as if my standing guard in the darkness would prevent his nightmares from entering the room.

At some point, I fail as a guard, and a dark room is in my dream, a dark room full of people trying to sleep, but the room is so packed that not everyone can lie down, and people are climbing the walls to sleep, climbing the walls or lying on top of other sleepers.

* * *

It's still dark when Majid's alarm goes off. He bolts out of bed. 'You better get back to your room and get ready,' he says. He pauses for a moment, kisses me sweetly on the lips, and heads for the shower.

The weight of my hangover presses down on me as I attempt upwards motion. Getting dressed is daunting. My feet get tangled in my pants. I look for a glass of water on the room-service table, but this involves viewing and smelling last night's food. The thick white of the sour cream turns my stomach, and I rush out of the room before it coaxes up the vodka and caviar mixture within.

Back in my room I open the windows that lead out on to the roof and breathe in the cool, diesel-tinged air. It's definitely a Vicodin day. I swallow one from my dwindling supply. Adderall, too, and more water for my thickened tongue.

I still feel nervous and dizzy from last night's swirling nightmares, but when I enter the hair and make-up room and let myself be patted and daubed and stroked by Lily and Radovan, I feel the gentle narcotic euphoria rise on its incoming tide, lapping away at my hangover, which is a very good thing, because today I'm to mount a horse.

* * *

The horse's name is Gleb. Gleb's a little nervous. I think he's a bit camera shy, or maybe it's the hulking lights and dazzling reflectors that he doesn't like. I look him in the eyes and pet his nose. 'Hello, Gleb,' I say. 'Nice to meet you. I'm going to be riding you today. Don't worry about the camera. You'll be fine.'

He's a beautiful bay, and the smell of his freshly brushed coat is soothing to me.

I'm on my pony, Pete. Following the large hindquarters of Dad's horse. Ben Ho is on his pony beside me. Goldy. Goldy and Pete are friends. They like to be together.

Dad doesn't say much, he just leads the way, but this is the closest we ever get to him. The sound of hooves on earth and stones, wind in leaves, forest-filtered sunlight. The smell of horse sweat and oiled leather. My feet in the stirrups. Pete's slightly swaying motion between my legs. We're five years old, six years old, seven . . .

At eleven we're allowed to ride by ourselves, and whenever we reach a flat place or an open field, we race, and to gallop feels so free, and it's like a secret we share with our ponies, how good this feels.

'Meade, are you ready?'

Majid approaches me, and at his side is a guy who looks like a deranged Jesus. Tangled hair and beard surround deep-set, shadowed eyes. He's wearing a coarse tunic.

'Yeah, I'm ready.' I look into Majid's eyes and already there are the secrets that we share in there. And his secrets, seeping out.

'I want you to meet Dmitri. He's going to be in this shot.'

I reach out to shake his hand. He has very long, brown-stained fingernails and ropey veins. I'm pretty sure he's high. 'Hi, Dmitri.' I try to assess his drug choice. His grip is firm and his palms are clammy.

'Hello,' he says with a phlegmy 'h'.

Majid gets Dmitri situated on the front stoop of St Isaac's Cathedral. Homeless Jesus, expelled Jesus.

Today I'm wearing thigh-high boots, knit tights and a long jacket. Majid holds the reins while I mount.

'You know how to ride, right? Are you comfortable on this horse?'

'Yes.' I feel Gleb relax between my legs.

'I'd like you to walk him around the cathedral and then bring his speed up so that you come around this side of the church at a gallop.'

'Okay.'

Gleb and I start off around the church. I feel his twitchy muscles, wanting to run. I bring him into a trot, then a canter. Glee spreads through my limbs, and then we hit a full gallop, his metal shoes ringing on the pavement, and as we come around the front, the church bells go off. Gleb bucks, but I stay on him, and we fly past crouching Jesus, who I think has the nods.

I slow Gleb down, turn around and check in with Majid. One of the assistants is trying to rouse Jesus.

'Great, Meade,' says Majid. 'But I want you to do it again. This time, don't smile.'

I hadn't realized that I was smiling.

We round the church again and again, a lone-horse merry-go-round.

* * *

On the night flight back to Paris I have the seat next to Majid in a two-seat row, which allows me to make this a one-Xanax rather than a two-Xanax trip. He seems to sense my anxiety. He takes my hand and kneads my palm with his thumb.

I study the full curve of his upper lip, a shape that I've only seen in statues, in the Greek and Roman gods section at the Met. Dad's favourite room. He gets ideas for his plastic surgery in there. Those straight noses, the resolute chins.

Sitting on the runway is the hardest part. Maybe if I could be kissing those lips, disappearing inside his mouth, I could forget the jet stagnation. But it doesn't really seem cool with Michael and Lily across the aisle from us. So I close my eyes and focus on his thumb.

It's such a relief when we finally barrel down the runway and lift off. The stewardess brings us red wine, and when we reach cruising altitude, I achieve a state of non-panic.

'Come home with me.' Softly, in my ear, his warm-breathed words.

But I can't. 'I have to get home. I haven't been able to reach Ben at all. Tomorrow?'

He doesn't answer.

Throughout the plane, everyone has turned off their

lights, everyone is sleeping. Majid rustles through the plastic bag of flight accoutrements. He pulls out an eye mask and tears the cellophane wrapping with his teeth. He takes the mask and slides it over my head. I have a brief moment of freak-out, but the sliding gesture is so sensual, his fingers encircling my skull, that I can take it, and the forced darkness envelops me, isolating me from all else but his fingers, my hair, and thick white jet noise.

Alone, on the taxi ride home, I watch the feeble morning sun slowly suffocate under a white blanket. I want to crawl under my own blankets, so so tired, residual Xanax heavily dictating the horizontal position. But instead, after my driver, a small man with sleepy eyes, lifts my luggage from the trunk, it's up to me to get it through the door and up the stairs. I hit the buzzer to our apartment from the front door, on the off-chance that Ben Ho will get out of bed and help me, but I don't hold a lot of hope for this at five in the morning.

So I clunk my way up solo, ready to count myself among the sleeping. Maybe I'll slip into Ben Ho's bed.

When I enter the apartment I immediately feel the void; no, the violation. We've been robbed, I'm sure of it. Objects are missing. The clutter of the entrance is gone, but I can't even take it in, can't assess, because the fear hits me: What if the intruder is still here?

I leave the door open behind me and am grateful for the arrangement of rooms. Ben Ho's bedroom is the first on the left. I tiptoe in to wake him.

His bed is empty. Empty, and made. Making his bed is not a habit of his. Usually it's more of a nest that he scatters with belongings. Piles of clothes, drawings, rolling pencils, bottles of water.

A thief wouldn't make a bed. Maybe Ben Ho had a delirious cleaning spree, stayed up all night. In the living room; he must be making something.

But the living room, I discover, is empty. Empty of his easel, empty of his scraps, empty of him.

My heartbeat clogs my ears and I stumble across the room like a drunk, banging into furniture. A piece of paper flutters to my feet. I snatch it up, desperate for it to be a drawing, a doodle. But it's too clean, too. Just a row of neatly formed words, words that say, 'Moved in with Linda for a while,' and 'hope the Russia trip was –'

Somehow I'm on the floor. A broken piece of pencil lead on the rug is all that I can see, a giant craggy thing, a graphite landscape.

* * *

I'm yanked from the chasm of unconsciousness by a small, rough tongue licking patiently on my cheek. I open my eyes and am face to face with a miniature schnauzer who stares at me from beneath his grey brow.

'Henri! Viens ici! Henri!' A distant voice. The voice of an old woman. It gains volume, it approaches. 'Henri! Maintenant!' Solid, hard-soled shoes on the floor beside me. A gasp. A gnarled hand grasping me, gently shaking me. 'Mademoiselle, ça va?'

I twist around to look at her, and she's staring at me from beneath grey bangs. She's tiny, too, and has bright eyes the colour of an espresso bean. She starts chattering away at me, in far too rapid French for me to decode. She tries to lift me, but obviously that's not going to work. She must weigh all of eighty pounds.

The schnauzer trots in semicircles back and forth around me, his little pointed ears tilted forwards as I prop myself on my elbow and gradually sit up. The woman feels my forehead.

I search in my mind first for what happened to me. I fainted? I hyperventilated? I don't know how to say either word in French.

'Mon jumeau est parti,' I finally say.

He left. He's gone.

She says pretty words, soft words, and takes me by the hand. I find myself being tucked into my bed, and a few minutes later, she's handing me a cup of camomile tea. The schnauzer jumps up on the bed beside me.

'Henri! Non!' But she laughs as she scoops him up in her withered arms.

'Merci. Merci.' It's all I can think of to say. My mind feels like clogged gears, and I can't even remember how to ask her her name.

* * *

When I walk through the courtyard of the École des Beaux-Arts, clusters of students hang around the fountain and laugh and play bongos and eat sandwiches, and I feel nothing in common with them, no sense of moving through life with them, of even being alive.

Two reverberating rings from the bell tower: it's two o'clock, and he'll be walking out of his art-history class. I climb the dusty stairwell and wait outside his classroom door where I hear the scraping of gathered books and the clenching teeth of backpack zippers. Voices, a multi-chorded progression of them, and I recognize his note within the chords.

The door bursts open. I see his head rising above the pack. He's looking unwaveringly at me, as if he had seen me before the door opened.

'Hi, Meade. You want to go get a coffee?'

The remaining pieces of me can't speak. He takes me by the hand, apparently I do have a hand, and we start walking.

Holding hands, walking through the hallways of school for the first time, the linoleum floors of St George's Pre-School, three years old, on our way to sing songs while Miss Jackie plays the piano. 'This land is your land, this land is my land . . .'

* * *

I watch him order coffees, watch him stir in two cubes of sugar. His mobile phone on the table, the phone that he never answers, says 2.22.

'Stop being so melodramatic, Meade. Talk. I know you can talk.'

He releases my voice. 'Is this all because I hit Linda? Because I promise I'll never do it again.' Of course it would help if she didn't have one of those little-girl voices that just make you want to smack her.

'Look, Meade, we've always been together. Always.'

'Yeah, that's right. As we should be.'

'I need to be . . . a little more independent.'

'You're not being independent. You're just going from me to her.'

'It's more than that . . .'

'Please come home.' But I see it in his eyes, he's got the gates up. Well, more like a picket fence and I can peek through the gaps, but still, a barrier, a property line.

'I don't think I'm doing you any good, either. I can't make you eat, I can't get you to stop taking all your little pills –'

'Don't make this out like you're doing me some favour, because you're not.' I smash my fist on the table, harder than I realized, and the coffee cups jump up from their saucers. My hand hurts, which makes me feel strangely better.

'You can be such a fucking bitch,' he says calmly. He

puts a cigarette in his mouth, lights it, and then inserts it carefully between my lips.

I suck smoke.

★ ★ ★

I need arms to hold me, a tongue to lick my wounds. And I'll lick his wounds too, wherever they may be.

I can't spend the night alone in this apartment, that's for sure. A double dose of painkillers and hours spent in the foetal position, thumb in mouth, have brought me no comfort. I was never meant to be alone. After a shot of whisky I call Majid.

★ ★ ★

Crouching at the top of Notre-Dame, an illuminated group of gargoyles points and laughs at me. The bridges are like stitches which bind the gash that cuts Paris in half, and I cross to the other side.

While crossing I feel nervous, ungrounded, and if I look at the river, swollen and dark, so high that the steps that normally lead down to an embankment now lead directly into the water, I actually feel my body being swept into its current, and I'm afraid, so I look straight ahead and walk in the centre of the bridge.

It's easy to find his building, right on the *quai* in the sixth.

He's on the sixth floor, but there's no way I'm going to close myself into a tiny elevator right now, so I walk up the stairs, breathless before I even start. I have to force myself to gasp at the musty air, which tastes of the river.

When he opens the door he says, 'What's wrong?', so I guess I must look weird. He pulls me into his arms, though, which is the best thing he could do, and the Seiney air starts to go a little deeper inside of me.

Finally I say it. 'Ben Ho left me.'

'Come sit down.' He leads me into the living room, a surprisingly blank, white room where I find myself sitting on a low, white couch beneath a high, beamed ceiling. 'What do you mean, he left you?'

'He moved out.'

'Why?'

'I think mostly because I punched his girlfriend.'

He laughs. 'Oh, I see.' He's laughing at me. 'Why did you do that?'

I don't know how to explain it. 'Hmmm?' he says, and he tucks a strand of my hair behind my ear.

'I just – couldn't resist the impulse. I didn't think about it. My fist flew in her direction. What's scary about it is how satisfying it was.'

He kisses my hand, the same hand that made itself into a Linda-punching fist. 'Maybe you need to learn a little self-control.'

'Maybe I do.'

But it's not at all self-control that follows. I don't even know how I end up flat on my back, sandwiched between him and the couch. I think it's his fingers inside me that are making me come, I open my eyes and his are right there, but everything is blurry. It's his fingers, yes, and then my own fingers curl into a fist.

* * *

I wake up and can't remember where I am, and for a moment he's a stranger to me, the man lying in bed next to me, his arm slung across my body, trapping me. I fling his arm off and sit up, looking out at the terrifyingly unknown room, too much white, nothing for my mind to grab on to, my heart stampeding, the man sleeping, calmly breathing, and then the realization: this is Majid, I am in Majid's bed, in Majid's apartment.

But this doesn't stop my crashing heart, and I have no idea where Ben Ho is, where my twin is sleeping, where *she* lives.

I'm going to have a heart attack. I'll die on white sheets and Majid will wake up and find me. And my soul will be released, and I'll be back in the womb with Ben Ho. I smooth my hair, fold my hands over my chest and wait to die, but I become so calm at this thought that my heart-beat returns to its normal, sluggish state, and I don't die. So I get up and have a cigarette.

* * *

Sleep is not an option, even with Xanax. Maybe a bath. And I can scope out the bathroom while he's sleeping. That's where you really discover things about people. It's the soul of the home, where you look yourself in the eyes, where you wash off the outer world, where you dispose of your waste, where you keep your pills.

Maybe there's some high-powered sleep inducers in there, some nightmare slayers. He wouldn't mind if I took one. Or two.

I tiptoe in and turn on the light, revealing a vastness of gleaming white marble with grey veins. It's so clean and neat that at first glance there are no indicators of his presence in here, except a black toothbrush. Natural bristles. The medicine cabinet has a frosted-glass door with art deco patterns around the edges. I open it carefully in case it squeaks, but it moves smoothly on its hinges.

I can't tell what the pills are. And there are some pills, three bottles of them, but he's removed them from their commercial packaging and stored them in what looks like early twentieth-century pharmaceutical jars. And the pills themselves don't have the familiar markings of my American brands. No telling embossed logos. Just smallish white pills, larger whites that are round and have flat sides, and an enticing-looking yellow pill, thin but slightly convex.

I consider taking the yellow. Maybe it's for sunshiny dreams.

There are drawers, though. I open the top drawer. A razor, cedar-scented shaving cream in a silver tube. A whitening toothpaste. I squeeze a little on to my finger. It's bright red. Rub it on to my teeth and rinse. There's a wide-toothed comb, a small Mason Pearson brush. Dental floss. Next drawer: very sharp fingernail scissors. Shea-butter body lotion. Acqua di Parma cologne, a bright blue liquid that smells of things oceanic. A travel-sized sewing kit with extra buttons. And then I reach into the back of the drawer and find a tiny green phial. Which contains a powdery substance. This looks promising.

Coke, I guess. I've never tried it before. I've always gone for the labelled, the controlled. But I'd like to feel what he likes to feel. I go back into the bedroom to make sure he's still asleep. I listen to the soft rhythm of his breathing and gently kiss his cheek. His breathing pattern remains smooth and steady, a calming loop.

I'm just going to try a little bit. I guess I'll need a snorting utensil, so I take a twenty-euro note from my purse and roll it up. A credit card, too, to form it into a line. I saw *Scarface*, I know what to do. I pour a wee bit of the powder on to the marble counter, scrape it into formation, and vacuum it into my sinus cavity. The phial returns to its home in the back of the drawer.

In the living room I light another cigarette and wait to see what happens. It doesn't take long, just a one-cigarette time unit. I feel it spread joyously through my cells, and I don't think this is coke, because it's making me want to lie down. We're talking narcotics here. I recognize a loyal friend. But this is a more immediate and intense friendship, a remarkably comforting friend who caresses me and whispers to me of love.

'Yes,' I whisper back. 'I love you, too.'

I slip into bed with Majid and he rolls over and wraps his warm body around me, a living cocoon, and I think of those strange creatures who live underneath ice in the deepest, darkest waters of Antarctica, clinging to the magnetic pull of the bottom of the earth, wiggling luminously, sketching colourful shapes in the darkness with their internal glow. I float, suspended, beside them.

Purple-green sea plants sprout from my calves, and then my thighs, and their tendrils sway to the pulse of the deep.

★ ★ ★

The next morning my nerve endings feel raw. Each sound I hear is an assault: the war between china and wood as Majid sets down a cup of coffee on the night table for me.

'Good morning,' he says. 'Did you sleep well?'

Morning doesn't seem to faze him. He smells of his cedar shaving cream and his seaside cologne. I remember something about the sea . . . I need sunglasses to deal with the whiteness of his shirt.

'Ummm, I woke up for a while in the middle of the night. But the sleeping parts were good.' The green phial. I wonder if that's part of his morning routine? I look into his eyes to see if his pupils are dilated, but his eyes are so dark that it's hard to tell.

'You should have woken me up. I would have seduced you back into sleep.' He smiles as he hands me the cup of coffee. Even his teeth are too bright for me. His movements are smooth and alert. Maybe it's that yellow pill, maybe that's the morning solution.

I sip the coffee, which is liquid, which is good, but it's too heavy, too aggressive, barrelling its way down into my stomach, and I'm afraid it's going to barrel its way back up. I attempt a peaceful smile and let my head sink back on to the pillow. 'Thanks.'

'*Ce n'est rien.* I've got to go to the studio now, but I'm going to leave you a key, and you can take your time. Do you have appointments today?'

'Yeah, I have a ten-o'clock.'

He kisses me again, then tugs the sheet down and kisses me some more. 'I'll call you later,' he says after he's removed his mouth from my breast, and he moves athletically out of the bedroom, and I hear him as he crosses the finish line of the front door.

'Bye,' I say to the shutting door.

* * *

I only took a little bit more, a recipe experiment to see how the powder mixes with Adderall. And it turns out to be a really good recipe. I have Adderall energy, and the powder works as an anaesthesia, almost completely numbing the severing of Ben Ho. No one even seems to notice that half of me is missing.

The desk people are unusually kind to me, giving me golden retriever gazes, and Marie-Hélène says, 'Baby, you look *superbe*! You have lost some weight?'

I'm graceful and light, skinny and beautiful, in love with all people, content. I hardly need food any more. 'I think so, yeah.'

And then she shows me the magazine, and I see page after page of my glossy self staring back at me, smooth-skinned and radiant.

I'm not afraid of the river today, and when I walk out on to the rue de Rivoli I head straight for the Seine where the sun is kissing its green face, and along the banks people smile when they see me, and I walk underneath a bridge and find three men living there; they have a bed and a desk, books and a bottle of wine, bearded faces and long hair, three wise men, and they give me a sip of their wine and let me lie down beside them and close my eyes.

* * *

A tortuously bright light sears through my eyelids. Where am I? Floodlights and an amplified voice. The voice echoes, bouncing off the underbelly of the bridge. It's a Bateau Mouche, the trawling, floating tour that thankfully passes on by.

I'm on a damp bed. I remember now, the three men. I sit up and look around me as the punishing beams recede. The men are still here. Two of them are playing chess, and one of them is looking through my portfolio. He runs his fingers thoughtfully through his matted beard. One of the chess players notices me. 'Elle se reveille,' he says to his friends. The guy looking at my photos closes my book and asks me, 'Ça va, mademoiselle?'

I reach into my pocket for my cellphone, to see what time it is, but my batteries are out.

'Vous avez faim?' One of the chess players offers me a chunk of bread and some wine. A wave of nausea sweeps over me, and the edges of my vision flutter, the warning flag of an excruciating headache. I try to concentrate on one focal point to ignore the heaving periphery, so I look at their chess pieces, worn and dirty little ivory statues. One of the points on the crown of the white queen is broken, and the centre of her is cracked. I start to cry, and the three men huddle around me, a human fortress. One of them is still holding the bread.

Inside their fortress words start spewing out of me. 'J'ai peur. J'ai une honte si profonde en moi . . . un monstre avec des tentacules pointues, glissantes, qui poussent et se multiplient. J'en suis pleines, donc je n'ai pas faim.'[1]

The three of them look at me in a kind silence with their bloodshot eyes.

Finally, one of them hands me the wine and says, 'En ce cas, buvez!'

I drink. I drink until all I can manage to say is, 'Taxi?' The guy who had been looking at my portfolio stands

---

1. 'I'm scared. I have a shame so deep inside of me . . . a monster with pointed and slippery tentacles that grow and multiply. I'm full of them, so I'm not hungry.'

and gathers up my book and my purse and offers me his arm. I grab on to the greasy brown corduroy of his jacket, and we begin to walk. 'Au revoir,' say the chess players, and they turn back to their game.

As we approach the stairway to the street, I have to stop to throw up. I lean over the banister and produce a retched trickle of bile. The man stands politely waiting for me. I throw up three times before we reach the taxi stand. I find myself in a black car with Arabic music singing out from the speakers. He hands me my portfolio and my purse. I look inside the purse, to give him something. The first thing my hand touches is my rolled-up twenty-euro note. Oh yeah. That. I unroll it and offer it to him.

His accepting fingers are stained yellow. 'Merci. Bon courage.' When he closes the door, the wavering voice in the speakers throws me into confusion for a moment as I search my mind for the address, the address of the empty apartment.

* * *

Except the apartment isn't empty. When I walk through the door I smell cigarettes, both the burning one and the butts I find populating the ashtray in front of Ben Ho, surrounded by piles of his scribbly drawings. A half-empty whisky bottle serves as a paperweight for the drawing he's working on now. He looks up, pen in hand, cigarette in mouth, and the circles under his eyes look like ink smears.

I wait for him to say something, but he just slowly sets down his pen, leaves the cigarette burning in the ashtray, rises up out of his chair and faces me.

Tears sluice down my face as I run at him, lay my head on his shoulder, and hold on to a piece of his hair. He clenches me so that our chests are pressed together, and I feel our hearts lunge at each other in a perfectly synchronized, rapid-fire beat. I grab a strand of my own hair and offer it to him. He takes it, and as he brushes it back and forth across his whiskery cheek, our heartbeats slow down. Then he drops the strand, grabs me by the shoulders and backs away.

I breathe in the whisky fumes of his sigh.

'Where've you been? I came by last night to check on you, and you never showed up. Your phone's turned off, too.' He stares me down with his ink-blot eyes.

This is not quite the avowal-to-come-back greeting that I had hoped for, but at least he's here, at least he's worried about me. I realize that my jaw is sore, I've been clenching my teeth so hard. With an effort, I open my mouth and say, 'I spent the night with Majid.'

He looks at me blankly for a moment. 'That guy? He's too old for you.'

'He's not so old.'

'How old is he?'

'I don't know.'

'See! I bet you he's –'

'But what does that matter, anyway? It's more about the quality of the person. That's what you've always said.'

Ben Ho sits back down and sloshes some more whisky into his glass. He holds it up to the light for a moment before he pours it down his throat. Finally he mutters, 'I don't quite trust that guy.'

'Why not?'

'I don't know. He's just a little too smooth. There's got to be something jagged behind it.'

'He was a political prisoner in Iran for three years. Starting when he was seventeen.'

'Oh. That's brutal.' He picks up his pen and starts making dark, jagged shapes. Drawing always calms him down. 'What happened to him there?'

'I don't know. He doesn't want to talk about it. But he screams in his sleep.'

'He was probably tortured.'

He draws an open mouth with bold lines coming out of it that taper off into shaky ends.

Just the word 'tortured', the thought of it happening to him, breaks over me with a fresh wave of nausea. My knees go slack, and I drop into one of the empirical chairs and hold on to its pillared arm. The cushion is gold.

'So where've you been tonight? You look like shit. You're getting too skinny, by the way.'

I light a cigarette and envision the three sets of bloodshot eyes. 'I spent the evening with some new friends.'

'Really? Well, that's good. You need to make some friends, not be alone so much.'

'Maybe I'll learn to play chess.'

'Yeah?' He draws black-and white-squares, a crown.

'Marie-Hélène thinks I look great, by the way.'

'She's warped.'

'I'm not as skinny as Linda.'

'You can't see yourself.'

I feel a little rush of pleasure at the thought that my bones might protrude more than hers.

I'm out of Vicodin. My head itches with anxiety. I look across the table at Majid and consider asking him if I can have some of his powder, but he's never mentioned its existence to me. I don't know when he's using it himself, but the level in the phial is dropping, and I don't think I can get away with taking any more of it without him noticing that I am a drug thief.

At breakfast I clutch my coffee cup. 'I'm nervous,' I say. I have a shoot with Max, the old German guy, today, an advertisement for shoes, and I feel like I'm about to be unfaithful.

'Why, my love?'

'Shooting with Max for the first time, I guess.' I spill a bit of coffee as I insert cup into saucer. 'Do you have anything for anxiety?' I ask hopefully. I scratch my head behind my ear like a dog.

'I have something,' he says, and as I wait for him to

produce the green phial, he grabs me by the back of the head and starts kissing me tonguely, and then he picks me up off of my chair and carries me into the bedroom, where he lays me down on the bed, and then it's hands, tongue, hands, penis; and while he's coming he grasps my throat, and in a state of non-breathing I come, too, and my anxiety drains away for a moment, but then my head still itches with its cellular craving of more euphoria.

* * *

Liquid Majid seeps secretly from me as I sit in the hairdresser's chair, watching myself in the mirror as an Asian guy with green hair standing out in spikes from his head, a Statue of Liberty crown, brushes my hair.

Suddenly he sets down his brush and looks at me with disgust. 'I'm not going to do your hair.'

'What?'

He picks up a comb, so I guess he was just kidding, but it hurts as he scrapes the fine teeth against my scalp. He thrusts the comb in front of me. 'Look! You have lice.'

And I see the translucent creature, with its dark spot inside of it, and what is that dark spot? Is it blood? My blood? It moves on the comb, it has legs, it has antennae, and the sound of my horror fills the room, and I can't stop screaming, as I can feel the swarm of them now, crawling on my head. 'GET THEM OFF OF ME!!!'

I smack my head over and over, trying to kill them.

Max appears and grabs my wrists. 'Stop it! What are you doing?'

'Lice are crawling all over my head!'

'Don't worry. They won't show up in the photos.'

I burst into tears, ruining my make-up. The make-up artist and hairdresser are both looking at me with hatred. 'I can't do it,' I say to Max.

'*Liebchen*, do you know what it would cost to have to reschedule this shoot?'

Everyone is crowded around me. I want to cut off my head to stop the itching.

A tiny Asian girl, an assistant to the hairdresser, I think, works her way towards me and holds my hand. She looks about twelve years old, with her black hair in a ponytail and her lips shining with pink lip gloss. 'I'll get them out for you,' she says in a very high, soft voice.

Max looks at his watch. The girl leads me back to the chair and produces a fine-toothed metal comb. I ransack my purse in search of my Xanax. I take three with no water.

'Okay, okay,' says Max. 'Everyone take a lunch break while the model is deloused.'

* * *

A community of parasites has established itself on me. I feel a deep shame in hosting them, in providing a blonde, forested scalpland for them.

There's a certain satisfaction in watching the sweet Asian girl hunt them down, capture and kill them, one by one. Finally she sets down her comb. 'I'll get the eggs, too, after the shoot,' she says kindly.

The eggs. It's all I can think of while I make seductive shapes with my legs, displaying red shoes. How long does it take them to hatch? Are they being born under the lights, their births documented in a Louboutin ad?

* * *

It's a long walk home. When I enter Majid's apartment, he approaches me, his arms spreading in preparation of embrace, and I say, 'Don't touch me! I may still be infested!'

'What?'

'I have lice.'

This statement is very effective. He doesn't touch me.

Wordlessly he pours a glass full of cognac and hands it to me. Then he's moving around the apartment, stripping the bed, yanking towels from racks, filling shopping bags marked with the labels of luxury, filling them with the colonies hidden in loops and weaves of cotton.

Then he sits me down on a wooden stool. He takes one of his photo loupes from a drawer and examines my head with its magnifying lens, section by section. I drink my cognac. He finds and destroys one egg.

'You're going to have to check me, now,' he says, handing me the loupe. 'And then I'll give you something that will calm you down.'

* * *

His head has not been colonized.

He makes mint tea, and my heart sinks at the thought that this may be his idea of what's going to calm me down. I think I'm beyond mint tea. I puff on a cigarette and try to be patient during the steeping.

He pours the tea into pretty etched glasses and hands one to me. 'This will keep your stomach settled,' he says. He hesitates a moment and gets those retinal scanners going on me. 'Can you be very secretive?'

'Absolutely. Secretiveness is one of my specialties.'

He reaches into his jeans pocket and pulls out the luscious green phial and a tiny silver spoon.

'What is it?' I ask.

'The essence of Afghan poppies,' he says. 'It's very strong. One spoonful is a beautiful thing. More, and you will be useless.' He fills the spoon and holds it to my nose.

After his spoonful, we kiss for a long time, licking the mint flavour from each other's mouths. When the flowers start to bloom, we lie down, and in his arms I can feel sunlight radiating from his olive skin. Then he begins to rub the soles of my feet, and I feel his sunlight travel up my body.

The last thing I remember him saying is, 'In Afghanistan the water is very precious and very pure, made of melted snow descending from mountains that pierce the sky.'

* * *

'Come on!'

Ben Ho grabs my hand and we start running up a winding staircase inside a tower, decaying and Gothic, and I'm not sure what we're running from, but I trust Ben Ho.

When we reach the top, whatever the emergency was

seems to have disappeared, and a triangle of light slashes the floor. And then I have a hairbrush in my hand, and I start brushing his hair, and as I brush it, it gets longer and longer, and it starts wrapping around me like the tentacles of an octopus, around my arms and legs at first, then my head, my neck, so that I can't see or feel or smell anything but his hair, and I'm blissed out.

Until consciousness slaps me in the face.

★ ★ ★

The bed is empty. In the kitchen is a note from Majid: 'Chérie. You were sleeping so peacefully, I didn't want to wake you. Have some breakfast. Bisous, M.' He left me a croissant and jam, and the espresso pot is loaded.

While the coffee shoots up its spout, I bite off the two ends of the croissant and chew each end twenty-two times, creating a landing pad for the coffee.

On the forty-fourth chew it occurs to me that Ben Ho was sending me a message. The tower, it must be the tower in Notre-Dame. He's going to meet me at the top of the tower.

I'm so excited that I can barely swallow my coffee and pill. I don't look at myself in the mirror before I go.

When I put on my jeans, though, I have a little spine rush when I fasten my belt and have to go a notch smaller.

Walking fast, sun oozing from the sky, my whole body releases a purifying sweat as I get closer and closer to the tower, to my twin.

The Twin Towers. That's what Dad used to call us because we're both so tall, so it felt like a personal attack when the airplanes knocked them down. We went to New York not long afterwards and saw the hole where they had once stood, demarcating the tip of the island. I cried. Ben Ho collected what rubble he could find outside the barriers.

Of course he wants to meet me in the tower.

* * *

I hadn't expected to have to wait in line, and it's agonizing. I'm surrounded by tourists, mostly other Americans, with their hamburger asses and their beer stomachs, and they even smell like grilling hamburgers in this heat, so that I have to take slow, deep breaths to avoid vomiting.

The other problem is the seven-euro entrance fee. I left the apartment so quickly, I didn't even bring my purse. I've only got four euros in my pocket, so I scan the crowd and try to decide who might give me three.

The dollar is so low now, so I listen for a British accent and approach the person to whom the accent belongs, who turns out to be a guy with a shaved head and a thirty-five-millimetre camera hanging around his neck.

'Excuse me,' I say, 'I hate to bother you, but I'm supposed to meet my brother up at the top, and I'm three euros short. Would you mind loaning them to me? I can pay you back after I see him.'

'Uh, all right then,' he says. He hands me the coins, which feel slightly sweaty.

'Thanks so much.'

'Hey, do you mind if I take your picture?' He's already taking off the lens cap.

'I don't care.' I drill his lens with my eyes. 'See you at the top.'

* * *

I walk faster than anybody else and have to weave my way through the waddling throngs. It looks just like the staircase in my dream, and along the way there are little artillery windows, in case you need a good sniper-firing position. My heart's clanging, vibrating my whole body.

I see his hair up ahead, and I rush to grab his hand, but his hand doesn't feel right, and a stranger turns to look at me. I drop the disappointing hand and climb more stairs, scanning and sniffing the crowd as I go.

When I reach the top I walk slowly, all the way around, so I don't miss him if he's crouching or something, but he's not here yet, so I wait.

The rush of Paris swoops out below me, but there's a sort of wire netting that makes me feel jailed. I guess it's to stop people from jumping. My stomach twitches at the thought, and I have to turn away from the view.

And I'm facing the British guy.

'Hello,' he says. 'Did you find your brother?'

'Not yet. I guess he's running late. If you give me your phone number, I can pay you back later.'

'Oh, I'm not worried about the money. But maybe we could get together and have a coffee?'

'Maybe.' I look over his head for Ben Ho.

'Are you here on holiday?' He offers me a cigarette, which I take even though I just had one. Suddenly I'm extremely nervous, waiting. I didn't think about time,

I just felt he would be here. But I think it was night time in the dream. Fuck.

This guy is looking at me like he's waiting for me to speak. 'What?'

'Are you all right?'

'Yeah,' I say, but everything goes dark and I have to sit down. I feel a hand support me as I drop to the ground. The blood in my body isn't travelling in all the right directions.

'Take a deep breath. Do you have vertigo?'

'Vertigo.'

'Put your head down.'

His hand again, gentle, and then I'm resting my head on my knees, which feels good, and the blood rivers are flowing better now, and gradually I can see again. I see shiny black boots stomp out a burning cigarette.

'Ça va, mademoiselle?' My eyes travel up the boots to the uniformed legs, torso, and the face underneath a cap. Gendarme.

'Ça va.' But the boots don't move.

The Brit hands me a bottle of water, which I sip until the water revives me and think how amazing it is that water has such power.

The guy says something to the gendarme and then they're lifting me, and tourist eyes are viewing me, a Japanese kid takes a picture, and I can't bear to be in this tower any more.

'Would you mind walking back down with me?' I ask the guy.

'Not at all.' I'm grateful for his gentlemanly grasping of my arm, and I let him lead me down the stairwell, around some corners, and into a café as the bells call out with their reassuring, mature voices.

In the café he asks me if I want a cup of tea, a sand-wich?

'I think I'd like a glass of red wine.'

He hesitates. 'Do you think that's a good idea?'

I don't even bother to answer that question. I smile, and he orders two glasses of wine.

* * *

After the wine, I become excruciatingly tired. My head begins to nod and my eyelids are heavy curtains. I force the curtains up and try to focus in on his brown eyes, which look sweet and intelligent.

'I guess I'm not a very interesting conversationalist.'

'No, no . . . it's not that. I don't know what's wrong with me. I think I need to lie down.'

* * *

So I find myself gripping him on another staircase, this one leading to the apartment I shared with Ben Ho, whom I'm hoping to find behind the door. As we ascend, the old woman neighbour and her schnauzer descend.

'Bonjour, mademoiselle,' she says, a little flustered.

'Bonjour, madame.'

She and her schnauzer both look at me askance as we pass.

Before I open the door I have a moment of hope, and I feel alert, but I know as soon as we step inside that he isn't here, and I'm completely leaden again.

The guy starts to kiss me, which seems problematic, but I lack any will at all right now. My body is in a state of disobedience to the simplest of my commands.

He pauses. 'What's your name?' he whispers.

I hear my voice say, 'Meade.'

'Mine's Harry.'

'Nice to meet you.'

Soon I'm lying on my bed enjoying the relief of gravity,

sinking down into the mattress as his body moves on top of mine. I stare up at my mobile and watch it spin lightly around.

* * *

He rolls his weight off of me and lies on my bed, and my mattress begins to form his shape as his heat transfers into its oil products, and these indentations throw my stomach into purging mode. I get to the bathroom just in time to shut the door behind me and throw up red wine. No lumps of food, just a pure, liquid vomit of a rather pleasant burgundy hue.

I feel the flatness, no, the now concaveness, of my stomach, stroking its comforting inwards-reaching shape while I brush my teeth. When I go back to my room, he's standing in his underwear smoking a cigarette and talking on his phone, and I'm consumed with an intense desire for him to vanish and to wash his seeping fluids, his sweat, his saliva, his semen, from my pores and portholes.

It's a Xanax-worthy wait as he laughs and makes plans and flicks his ash out the window, but I have the panic-inducing realization that my Xanax is in my purse, at Majid's, and that I am in fact completely drugless. Fuck. Fuck fuck fuck.

When he hangs up he smiles at me and begins to roll a hash cigarette, so I delay his departure time.

'Do you mind?' he asks, holding the halfy up to light.

'Not at all.'

A hash cloud-cover hangs from my ceiling. He hands the roll-up over to me and I savour the sweet taste of it, which fills me so satisfyingly. This is dinner for me tonight.

'Do you want to come with me to meet some friends for dinner?' he asks.

How strange that he should ask this when I'm so obviously feasting. 'Uh, no. But thanks.'

'Well, let me give you my number. Give me a call anytime. I'll be in Paris another three days.' He finds pen and paper on my desk and writes his number in dense, blocky handwriting. 'What's your number?' Pen poised.

'I don't know.'

'You don't know?'

'Too many digits in these Parisian phone numbers.'

'Oh. Well, why don't you give me a call right now, and I'll register it.'

I take a deep, hashy puff and hold it in for a moment, and then exhale a series of rings. Smoke doughnuts. 'I left my phone at my boyfriend's apartment.'

'Right then.'

Departure time.

* * *

'Where have you been.' He says it coldly, calmly, with dead-fish eyes looking at me.

I'm shaking, and I'm trying to think how to discreetly get into my purse to get a Xanax, but my purse and my phone are both sitting on the table, right in front of Majid, and he's hovering over them as if they're evidence, and I know I'm on trial, and I'm guilty of betrayal.

'I went to meet Ben Ho.' But I feel the burning shame seared into my skin, and I never saw Ben Ho.

'He was looking for you, too. Would you like to hear his messages?' He picks up my phone.

He was looking for me. My heart lunges, and I smile, but Majid is not smiling. His stillness bursts into action, and he twists my arm behind my back and drags me over to the couch, and I land face down on its woven surface, trying to formulate words, but each word that appears disappears again before I can shape it, and he's moving very quickly, and I feel my hands being tied together behind my back, and then there's silk around my mouth, gagging me, so I'm freed of speech anyway. I twist my head around to look at him, but I only see a momentary flash of his hands as he loops another silk thing, a scarf, I guess, over my eyes and ties it tightly at the back of my head. I think that maybe I should be afraid, but instead I succumb to my silence and darkness.

Silence broken by the parting of metal teeth. When he unzips my jeans, I feel a callous on one of his fingers as he slides them down my thighs and I am exposed.

When he releases the scarf from my mouth and slides it down around my neck, pulling on it with a soft pressure, my life is completely controlled by his hand. He could pull tighter, he could stop breath from entering my body, and as I imbibe the available oxygen, his presence, his anger, his love, his being making me not alone, I'm infused with life.

* * *

He doesn't ask me any more questions. I fall asleep peacefully captive in his arms, but it ends up being a night of duelling nightmares, with his screams waking me up right at the climactic moment of my dream, which had started out calmly, just my mother standing in a sunlit room with rose-patterned wallpaper, and she's looking at me, or at least her eyes drift in my general direction, and she's smiling. I don't know why I start punching her, but I do, over and over again, until I'm bashing her head into the wall, and heads bleed a lot, and hers bleeds to the point that I can no longer see her eyes and her blood spreads on the wall, merging with the roses in the wallpaper.

And then Majid is screaming and I have to wake him up to make it all stop. 'You were just dreaming,' I tell him, urgently, and it's almost hard to talk because my jaw is so sore from my own teeth-clenching. 'What were you dreaming about?'

He looks at me and speaks in his foreign tongue and cries.

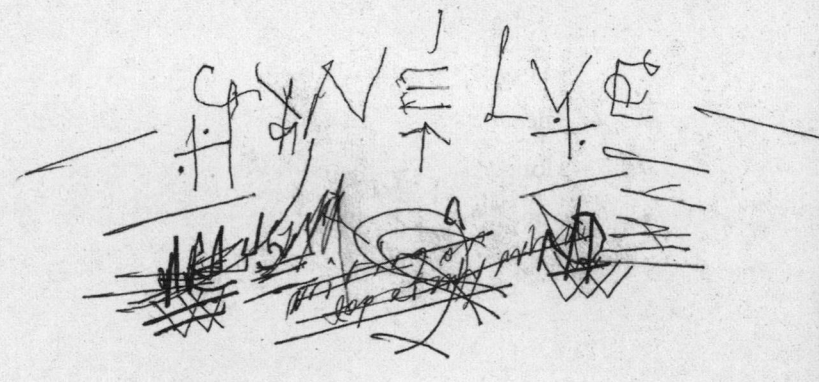

With a spoonful of poppies in my nose, I head out to meet Ben Ho. Linda's gone off to Italy for a long weekend, and Ben Ho actually called me now that the bitch is out of town. Maybe she'll be kidnapped in Rome or something. I imagine her kidnappers, two sweaty men with gold-capped teeth. They'll feed her a lot of lasagne and confine her to an apartment decorated in red, black and gold, and she'll get really fat.

I walk the contemplative monk's path with this vision in mind and then take the stairs up to the painting studio. When I enter the room, all the other people and junk in there jump away from my vision as my eyes, set on automatic focus, land on Ben Ho. He doesn't move, but when our eyes connect I feel like I'm stepping on to a conveyor belt that leads me straight to him. He puts his arms around me, draws me into his ribcage and kisses my cheek.

Then the other people reappear and I realize that they're

all standing around looking at Ben Ho's painting. I look at it, too. It's pretty gruesome. It's a woman who's being skinned; half of her face is peeled away from her skull.

Some guy says something about war victims and somebody else talks about surrealism. Ben Ho asks me, 'Do you know what that is?'

'I know what it is.'

'What do you think?' It's the Swiss guy. He offers me a cigarette and lights it for me.

'It's a woman getting a facelift.'

'Ahhh.' The Swiss guy edges closer to me, but I move towards Ben Ho.

'I'm doing a series,' he tells me. 'The next one is when the skin is stretched taut and the excess edges are being trimmed, and then the third one is right after it's sewn back on. Are you hungry?'

I'm not, and his painting is really unappetizing, but I want to be alone with him. 'Yeah.'

* * *

'Jesus fucking Christ, Meade. There's less and less of you every time I see you.'

'What do you mean?'

'You're getting so skinny. Pretty soon you'll disappear.'

'I don't think so. But maybe I'll get small enough that I can ride around inside your pocket, or live in your hair. I'll camp out on the highest spot on your head, and watch the world from there.'

'You'd get bored. Not to mention dirty, sometimes.'

'And at night, I'd curl up inside your ear. This part,' I reach over and touch the inner, shell-like curve, 'would make the perfect lounge chair.'

He laughs and picks up his menu. 'What do you want to eat? How about some *spaghetti aglio olio*. You like that.'

Spaghetti, olive oil, garlic, parsley, parmesan . . . all enemies.

I've gotten to where I can almost throw up at just the thought of food entering my body.

'Meade? Spaghetti?'

'Your painting is revolting.'

'Thank you.'

'It does kind of freak me out, that Dad does that. I mean, can you imagine doing that? It seems barbaric. Like when he uses that lever to rip the face off the skull.'

Ben Ho tucks his hair behind his lounge-chair ear. Ear

to ear, that's the slice that Dad makes. 'Well, that's part of the point. I don't think most people think of plastic surgery as the violent act that it is. Meticulous violence.'

'And when he pulls the skin tight and cuts off the excess with scissors? It's almost like trimming a piecrust. Or how about when he slices nipples and jams a saline blob into the opening?' I light a cigarette. 'Can we get some wine?'

Ben Ho makes effective waiter eye contact. He orders two spaghettis and a bottle of Chianti before I can even say anything.

'The liposuction,' I say. 'He marks the fat places with a Sharpie and then rummages around in the thigh or ass, pumping away with his vacuum cleaner, and you can hear all the globules of fat being sucked up, and why is the vacuum cleaner bag clear? You can see the horrible yellow, oily, lumpy liquid.'

The wine arrives, and that's a relief, but I go into a cold sweat at the thought of the *aglio olio*.

* * *

'Teens in exile can be a lonely breed,' says the German male model seated beside me on the Métro. The dark-haired teen on the other side of him nods. 'Come to a party with us. There will be dinner and other pleasant things.'

I certainly don't need more to eat, but the other pleasant things sound enticing, so I find myself walking between them, Jürgen and Stefan. The three of us have matching long strides. We walk alongside a wall taller than we are, so I can't see what's behind it.

The door that we arrive at has no address on it. It's made of metal and looks like a bank vault, except that it's covered in graffiti. The Arabic letters are prettiest. The door opens as two laughing girls emerge and we go inside.

Jürgen introduces me to the host, Rafi, who is a pale-skinned Spaniard with a gap tooth and large glasses. It's his night, his party after his show, and this is his atelier. He's all aglow, so much so that I feel my own spirits rise up my spine from my tailbone.

The room is large and without interior walls and has a storefront window, now blocked by metal caging. I follow Rafi through a cluster of older guys, uniformly thin and pierced, to the back, where masses of patterns hang on a rack next to a row of sturdy old sewing machines. 'Would you like some punch?' he asks me. 'It's a family recipe.'

Gathered around the punchbowl are smiling models,

not a common sight. In the corner, a DJ is choosing his next record. I sip some punch, and it tastes of fresh strawberries and oranges.

One of the smiling models leans into me and says, 'MDMA is the secret ingredient.' I down my glass.

* * *

Sitting on the couch with a bunch of other models, like a pile of puppies, I turn and look into the dilated pupils of Jürgen, whose lap I'm half sitting on. I don't know how I didn't notice when I saw him in the Métro, but he looks exactly like a girl. Not just any girl. He looks like me. My lips, my face shape, my hair, my eyes stare back at me. He sees it too. He smiles, showing teeth more vampirish than mine, and we look at each other unflinchingly, lovingly. Three or four songs move across the room from the turntable, touching the ceiling, touching the floor.

'Meine Zwillinge,' he says.

I remember that word. 'I already have a twin.'

'Do you want to hear a poem?'

'Sure.'

'It's in German.'

The image of Sylvia, the German au pair who took care

of me and Ben Ho when we were three or four, floods my
brain. I see her green eyes and very straight, chin-length
light brown hair. Her skin is milky, her teeth crooked.
There's a scar on the index finger of her right hand.

'Go ahead,' I say.

He puts his mouth next to my ear.

> Da hab' ich Angst vor,
> Sagte mir einmal ein Freund,
> Meinerseits Schueler,
> Seinerseits Mentor,
> Ein Mensch.

> Ist es die Angst vor dem Leben,
> Zu wissen, dass man lebt,
> Wie man lebt,
> Liebt,
> Stirbt.

> Die Angst vor der Kunst,
> Die Angst vor der Kunst,
> Kunst,
> Künstler,
> Künstlerisch,
> Intentional orientiert,

Unorientiert,
Metaintentional Überorientiert.

Wenn wir uns finden,
Sehen wir uns wieder?[2]

'Apfelsaft, crayon drawings, Sylvia giving us a bath. Live, love, die. Little wooden rabbit and chicken ornaments for the Easter tree. Fear. Mr Potato Head. Sylvia liked his moustache.'

He nods at me as if this makes sense.

Ben Ho and I ended up speaking some weird version of our own of German, and Sylvia was sent back to Germany.

Stefan climbs over me and starts kissing Jürgen. I watch them for a while. There must be a time lapse in my brain because I can see trails of the movement of their heads. I almost feel like Jürgen's mouth is mine, and as I'm thinking of this, Stefan begins to kiss me. His mouth feels

2. 'I'm so scared of that, / A friend once told me. / I was a student, / He was a mentor, / A human being. // Maybe it's fear of life / To know that we live, / How we live, / Love, / Die. // Fear of art, / Fear of art, / Art, / Artist, / Artistic, / Intentionally oriented, / Unoriented, / Metaintentionally overoriented. // If we find each other, / Will we see each other again?'(Excerpt of poem by Paul Boche. Translation Hollis Hampton-Jones and Elena Rohrmoser.)

entirely different from Majid's. His tongue lacks the control and subtlety. I disengage, look at Jürgen one more time, touch my nose to his nose and say, 'Gute Nacht.'

* * *

I haven't heard German in all these years and on the cab ride home my mind is swimming with words, and I don't know what's German and what's my language with Ben Ho. *Schwimmen, schwimmen gehen, Wasser, warum, vrum, uns, ickendick, vistdu?, ickvill toosahmen sign* . . .

Immer.

When I get home Majid is awake even though the sun is beginning to creep up, and birds are making their frightening utterances. He has a book on his lap, and he looks up at me like my own thoughts are words on a page.

'What are you reading?'

'Poetry. Some Persian poems.'

I ask him if he'll read them to me and he does and I close my eyes and feel a meaning.

* * *

It's Sunday, and Majid had planned a picnic for us. Apparently picnics are a big deal in Iran, and it's a part of his culture that he seems to miss. But this picnic is not to be. I'm curled up on the couch wearing his sweater and watching the display outside. A spectacular lightning bolt flashes showily. It looks like the arteries of a god, and I think of all those erotic tales about Zeus coming to Earth and fucking mortals.

Which seems like the perfect occupation for the afternoon. But Majid is edgy. He's pacing, and I notice him squeezing his hands into tight little balls. The thunder makes its delayed timpani solo.

'It's a beautiful storm. We can have our picnic in here.'

'I can't eat. I don't like electrical storms.'

'Why not?'

The thunder makes a fantastically loud boom, and Majid looks as freaked out as Dad's English setter, Graham, during storms. There's no other word for it: he's cowering.

So I pet him. I pet behind his ears, up along his temples, the back of his neck. Another bolt crackles, and I dread the follow-up boom.

He's got a weird look in his eyes like he's somewhere else. 'Three,' he says. His whole body is trembling.

'Three? Three what?' I keep petting.

'تيرباران ها'

'In English?'

He looks at me, opens his mouth, and then swallows his words. I move my hand back to his temples, and I can feel him being slightly lulled. After a moment he reaches into his pocket and pulls out the phial. He seems more present in the room. 'We'll have just a bit,' he says.

'Sure.'

* * *

I watch his hands relax. I watch them feel the silken texture of the rope. I watch them adroitly tie a slip-knot, and I feel him slide it over my head. He looks me in the eyes while he calmly tightens it around my mortal neck, and then he blindfolds me.

Even through the blindfold I can see the strobe of lightning, and for a moment, I see my lit self, with only my eyes and my neck dressed. Questions flash through my mind: Where does my pleasure come from? Why does he like to do this to me? But I don't want to think about it. To be analytical about sex is to kill its power, and the questions disappear into the ions. I smell him and I feel his presence inside of me with a deep acceptance.

Behind my mask, behind my eyelids, visions float by, until one static image appears. A spiky-furred wolf stares at me with yellow eyes, and I stare back at him. He bares his teeth. They look very sharp.

* * *

It's working. I am becoming smaller, and now the designers want me for their shows. I sit on a folding chair in a tent in a row with the other girls who have managed to achieve the body of a twelve-year-old boy who lives in a land without access to McDonald's. My hips are narrow, I've gotten my breasts to almost disappear, and I'm no longer sentenced to having a period.

Today is my first *défilé*, and this designer, Octavio, a permanently tanned Italian whose face has definitely been trimmed and sewn back on to his head a few times, is particularly known for choosing the thinnest girls. He doesn't even provide food for us for fear of our bloating stomachs distorting his dresses, but we're given B vitamins for energy. To be chosen by him, to fit into his strictly shaped designs, makes me feel indescribably proud. I have vanquished the insidiousness of fat. I trace my protruding left hip bone. When no one is looking, I slide my finger up my side, counting my ribs. I can feel each one with remarkable clarity.

I'm the only American girl who has achieved this state. The other girls in the row are all Eastern European or Russian, and had a head start due to limited food supplies during their childhoods. In their cases, their thinness was fated, whereas in mine, it was an act of will.

I sip champagne from a small glass funnel inserted into a single-serving bottle and celebrate my thighs that no longer spread their mass on the seat of the chair. I watch myself smoking in the mirror as the hairdresser, also one along a row of his kind, brushes my hair.

I feel like I'm moving through the kind of dream I often have, where there are lots of people around, but I don't really know them or why they're there, and the crowd keeps shifting, and they seem purposeful, but to me it's all just chaos and confusion that I watch from stillness. There's music playing, people are chattering in different languages, there's pre-show excitement. I concentrate really hard on the fact that I'm sitting on a chair. The chair has a plastic surface. Otherwise I'm afraid I'll float up out of my body and travel around the tent.

Champagne. Vitamin B. Xanax. I just have to let myself

be groomed and dressed, and then walk from point A to point B, stop, pose, turn, and walk from point B back to point A. I'm calm. Xanax is my friend. Never mind about all the people out there, packed tightly into the darkness. They're just part of a landscape. A narrow peninsula jutting into the people ocean. Xanax. Even the word is comforting. The symmetry of it. Backwards, forwards, all the same.

My hairdresser screams. He is freaking out. Eyes and mouth wide open. Not the lice again. Please not.

He holds up a sizeable hunk of hair. It takes me a moment to realize that the hair is mine. Was mine. It's now separate from my head. He throws it at me, lets his brush clatter on to the dressing table, turns away and lights a cigarette in one motion.

I didn't feel it come out. It's like it just dropped right off of my head. I feel my head to see if there's a bald spot, but I seem to have plenty of hair left. I throw the hunk of hair into the trashcan, this former piece of myself, and I drink some more champagne.

Somebody yells at my hairdresser, and he comes back and silently, with trembling hands, finishes up with the rest of my hair. You can't tell that there's any missing. He shapes it into a hair anvil.

Then I'm sent over to the racks of clothes, where a middle-aged woman dresses me like a doll, carefully matching all the accessories to a Polaroid she has for reference. For a moment I'm standing in my underwear in this room full of people, but she quickly helps me into a black dress so heavy with beadwork that it feels like armour. My thin pride dissipates as she struggles to zip it up. She taps my stomach and says, 'Suck in,' and after my solid diet of deprivation, clearly not enough deprivation, I hold my stomach in until she succeeds with the zipper. I can only take very shallow breaths.

I try to focus on reading the instructions that are posted for the models:

Be precious.

Seek the light.

Your glance is remote.

Mirrors are your friends.

You are a princess.

Look in the distance.

Grace and fluidity.

Be untouchable.

Be a diva.

My dresser's hands are moving hurriedly. Octavio stands up on the stairway leading to the runway and gives us a pep talk.

He snaps his fingers. 'It's all about attitude (snap), attitude (snap), attitude (snap). Everyone wants to be you, but they will never be. You know this. You are creatures of great beauty, wearing creations of great beauty. *Andiamo!*' He claps his hands together and bares his teeth in a bleached smile on his sun-soaked face.

After a hushed moment, the runway music starts. I'm third in line to go out. When the first girl does her thing and comes back, a small band of women claw her clothes off her and plunge her into the next outfit. The second girl is out on the peninsula now, and I'm up next. My heart ignores the rule of Xanax and begins pumping furiously. I wish I could have a sip of water, but there's no time. I'm on.

As I walk the runway, flicking my hips to the bass line, I can't see anyone, but I know they're out there, judging, scribbling in notebooks. I just keep moving, keep moving to the rhythm. Time seems both compressed and elongated. Finally or suddenly, I find myself at the end of the runway, and now it's a gangplank, and I stop at its dizzy-ing edge and strike my practised pose.

I hadn't counted on the bank of photographers and their simultaneous flashes. They set off an electrical storm in my head. I'm struck by lightning. It knocks me flat on to the ground. I can't move, but I feel the sick rush of speeding through a tunnel, a long, dark tunnel, and I'm careening towards the light.

* * *

'I've received many complaints about you.'

I sit across Marie-Hélène's desk from her, watching her red lipstick-ringed mouth say these words. Her lips form a dazzling variety of shape changes as she speaks, culminating with the round sucking-ready 'ou'. I don't say anything and wait for her lips to move some more.

'The other designers have all cancelled you.'

Again, very round.

'You are listening to me?'

Me. M-m-m-m-m. Top lip meets bottom lip. A greedy little sound.

'Meade?'

'Yes?'

'I hope you will not be further trouble. Perhaps you should take a small vacation. Rest. Be ready for your shoot with Majid next week.'

Vay-cay-shun. I like the two rhyming syllables, and the blast of air from the 'sh' suffocated by the 'n'.

'We cannot work with you if you continue to be unreliable.'

Her little pink tongue is so busy with those 'l's.

'You understand?'

'I understand.'

I really want to feel Majid's tongue in my mouth.

* * *

On the street my wilting body seems incapable of walking, so I lean against the post at the taxi stand to prop myself up, and a gleaming Mercedes taxi glides to a stop beside me. My hand reaches out to open the door. The door is heavy. The finality of its low thud of closure tingles through me. The driver's questioning eyes hang over the dashboard in the mirror, and to them I utter a number, a street name, before I lie down on the beaten and softened skin of the interior.

I feel the weight of the car pressing down on the asphalt, the heaviness of it making it roll smoothly along, and I have the sensation of riding in a mobile coffin. Not in an unpleasant way, not in a trapped way. It's a soothing voyage. A procession of street lamps marches solemnly by, while an uneven row of windows rushes behind them. When the rolling stops intermittently, people appear. Bodiless people. A succession of jostling heads, faces that I'll never see again, faces that don't see me, don't know that I exist. If I were in a coffin, would it be open? Would people peer in at the abandoned container of myself? A make-up artist would paint a faux blush of life on my cheeks, but underneath, the blood would not be flowing. Stagnant pools beneath.

* * *

I guess I fell asleep. I wake up from slaps on my cheeks and open my eyes to a looming face with blue-black, pocked skin. Three vertical scars point from his forehead to his nose. The eyes I recognize from the mirror. He's so close that I can feel the warm breeze of his exhalations and see the thin red tributaries in the yellows of his eyes.

'Mademoiselle, reveillez-vous. Mademoiselle.' His gums are a bright, dark pink, framing blastingly white teeth.

'I'm awake,' I say, and his face moves away. His sweat has a spicy smell.

'Dix-huits euros, s'il vous plaît.'

Money. Purse. Wallet. I remember these things. In my wallet I find a twenty and hand it to him. A flash of silver lights the edge of the bill for a moment before it disappears into his thin hand, the hand that then pulls me up and out of the car and leaves me on the street.

* * *

Majid's apartment is empty of him. I eat a cracker a tiny bite at a time, chewing each piece until it dissolves on my tongue so that it lasts longer. I wish Majid were inside my mouth instead of the cracker. I think come is a good low-calorie source of protein. In the bathroom drawer I find the powdered poppies and have one spoonful for dessert.

The bed invites me to lie down. I lean back on its fluffy pillows and watch a gathering rain out the window, droplet joined by droplet until a whole crowd of them is sliding down the windowpanes and a collective forms to join the river, to make it swell. I want to take a bath, but that would require moving. Behind my eyelids mysterious faces emerge, float across my eyeball, and disappear. The raindrops and I, the glass and I, the river and I, the bed, the faces, we are all indistinguishable from one another, which makes me happy.

A moment, an hour, maybe more, slides by and Majid becomes part of me, too, very directly, pushing and pushing his way inside. An ecstatic elevator rises up my spine.

'I know what you like,' he whispers in my ear, tickling me with his breath, and then his fingers span my throat, and when he takes my breath away, white stars are born, burn, and explode.

★ ★ ★

A shooting pain wakes me during the deep quiet of night. It's my hip bone, tired of its job of being part of my skeleton, and I can feel it spreading dissent to the rest of my bones, so that they all want to quit.

I've never felt bone pain before, but it is intense, and I think I better have some narcotics right away to squelch the uprising.

Majid lies sleeping beside me. I smell our mingling

come and his hot, liquory breath. I touch him to make sure
he's deeply asleep before I get back into the poppy jar.

Two spoonfuls this time. He might notice, but what
the hell. I drink a shot of cognac and smoke and wait for
my skeleton to cooperate.

A midnight-blue velvet curtain lowers slowly over the
pain.

*　*　*

Christened and anointed bells ring inside my head, their
sound waves searching out my cavities, vibrating my nasal
passages. I wonder what their names are. Mathieu? Pierre?
Voices growing rich and operatic with age. Metal tongues
clanging against the roofs of their gaping mouths.

'Meade?'

Surely they're not named 'Meade'.

'Meade?' Hands on my face and I open my eyes.

Again, a looming face, only this one belongs to Majid,
and his eyes caress.

'You better wake up. Don't you have shows to do?'

Shows. What would I be showing?

'Meade. The catwalk today. You don't want to be late.'

A sleek black cat walks on the edge of the rooftop.

'Meade? Drink some coffee.'

'I'm more of a dog person.'

'What?'

'No more catwalk for me.'

He hands me a small white cup of espresso. 'What are you talking about? You're booked for three shows today.'

'There were too many flashes going off. They knocked me down.'

He's quiet for a long time. On the rooftop, black cats, fluffy white ones, tiger-striped cats with ringed tails parade lightly on their paws with miraculous balance, fearless of the stony street below. He looks at his flame while he lights his cigarette.

A blue cloud emerges from his mouth and then he says, 'Just stick to print.'

* * *

Definitely not a cat. I'm a dog, an Afghan hound, and dogs need to walk, so after Majid leaves and I can't take the blankness, the whiteness, the emptiness of his apartment any more, I take to the streets with no leash and wander, wander.

I'm an ungroomed Afghan hound, my blonde hair

becoming matted as I avoid the brush, the brush that could remove hunks of me. The sky is a pale blue and Parisians look friendly today, like they want to pet me, but I don't end the pleasure of movement. I cross over the bridge to the Place de la Concorde, so deceptively beautiful with its globes of light all orbiting the obelisk, you can hardly imagine that this was the former setting for so many beheadings.

I see a crowd of orange people. Why are they all dressed in orange jumpsuits? And wearing white masks. Shouting from behind their masks. Behind them the gaudy flag with its stars and stripes, its red, white and blue, waves cheerfully from the top of a building, clashing with the orange. A really bad colour combination: red, white, blue and orange. In front of the building stiff soldiers hold machine guns. Beyond the orbits of the globes, a circle of those Ninja Turtle cops with their shelled bodies.

I'd like to have a shell.

I keep walking because it feels good to move.

In the Tuileries I sit for a while and stare at a statue of a woman until I see her breathing from her marble encasement where she lives patiently with outstretched, upturned arms. I sense her relief when the sun sets. Marble prefers moonlight. She sighs, and I buy a bottle of wine as I walk down to the river.

An Afghan hound living on powdered food, like an astronaut. One spoonful from my pocketed supply, and snorting I look at the sky and see a bird, an airplane and a helicopter in confluent but separate flight paths.

I land underneath a bridge and, as if time rides by without them, the same three bearded men remain how I last saw them, two of them playing chess and one lying on the bed. I wonder if they're really there or if this is a visual echo, but then they see me and greet me enthusiastically, each of them kissing me on my cheeks, and I on theirs, and each of their beards feels different against my skin. One is wiry, one coarse and stiff, and the last one is almost silky. I offer up my bottle of wine. I don't have an opener, but they do, and they even have small glasses that look clean. Only three though, so they give me my own and two of them share.

'Santé,' they say.

'Et enchanté,' adds Silky.

Wiry and Coarse go back to their chessboard. I know nothing about chess, but their concentration is so strong that it pulls me in and I can't stop looking at the board.

The squares begin to take on a third dimension, and when one of the ivory men finally travels, I feel like I'm moving with him.

Silky pulls a violin case out from underneath the bed, takes the violin out and sets the open case near the walkway. He tunes for a moment, and the sound of the strings reverberates underneath the bridge. He begins to play something mournful and yearning, achingly yearning, and twin rivulets of salted water slide down my face.

'I miss my brother,' I say to no one. I reach out and touch the sound as it moves from stone to water.

People walk by, and some of them drop coins in the case, and the thud of the coin momentarily disturbs the solemn beauty of the vibrating strings.

* * *

After a while the wine's all gone and I get cold, so I start to walk home on damply aching feet. I wish my feet could travel on warm sand instead of cold cement. Cement that used to be sand. Maybe I'm really walking on a beach in Anguilla. But the pervasive greyness, the invasive greyness, makes this impossible to imagine.

As I walk, Ben Ho's random cameras might see my scuffed boots, might see a thin strip of river decorating the stone banister of the bridge, puffs of carbon dioxide coughed up through an exhaust pipe, a plump white hand clutching the handle of a purse, the rapid movement of troops of conquering clouds. A sharp pinky toenail is slicing the edge of my large-headed fourth toe, so I sit down in a bus shelter, a bus shelter with the right number, eighty-two. Eighty-two is a number that will drive me home.

It begins to rain, but the bus shelter shelters me. I cough and wonder if my polluted exhalations are affecting the ozone layer. A gust of wind or maybe the cold breath of gargoyles pushes the rain into my shelter, showering me.

It's all right. I probably need a shower. A free hair wash.

The eighty-two arrives with the sighing sound of the compression of its brakes, and on the side of the bus is a huge picture of a girl who has just washed her hair, and the reflection of sunlight shines down its silken length. She looks at me calmly from beneath her mascaraed lashes for a moment before I realize she is me. She is the negative imprint of shadows and light on film bled on to paper in a very dark room.

Beyond the bleeding light, some digital master painter has transformed me into a creature with liquid pearls for skin, someone without pores, without stray hairs, someone with heaving breasts that I don't possess emerging from the neckline of a dress I would never wear.

The thrust of the levers that open the bus door startles me along with the impatient bus driver's 'Mademoiselle? Montez-vous?'

I climb.

* * *

Unable to bear being closed into the mirrored interior of the elevator in Majid's apartment building, I take the stairs. Slowly, slowly, I climb. The ceilings are so high that I pause on the landing of each floor to acclimate myself to the dwindling oxygen supply. I should have encampments at each level, a cot to lie on to avoid altitude sickness.

On the sixth floor, Majid's door. Deep, light-absorbent blue with a large gold knocking ring, a large gold knob.

I open the door into darkness. I guess he's still out.

A bath. The water in the bath will hold me in its warm embrace.

I don't see him, but then I smell him. Cedar, olive oil, mint. In the living room I hear him breathing. He's not asleep. Funny how sleep changes breath. My pupils enlarge and I see his huddled shape on the couch, his head resting on his clenched knees.

'Majid?'

The rotating gear of a lighter precedes soft illumin- ation, a burning candle. He looks up and I can see his skull, see the carved-out pools where his eyeballs rest. When he stands and moves towards me, I think he's going to hold me, but instead he pats me down like in an airport search until he runs his hand across the bump of the phial in my pocket, and then he slides his fingers down inside and removes it.

'You should just ask when you want some. Let me be in control of that. You don't want to become a junky.'

'Sorry.'

He holds my face by my chin and examines my eyes. After a moment, he lets go. 'I'll join you,' he says as he unscrews the tiny cap.

'Do you want to take a bath with me?'

He inhales a heaping spoonful, pauses for a moment of absorption and says, 'Why not?'

We go into the bathroom and I'm glad that I can rid myself of the clinging city. His bathtub is big, with a curved back on both sides and the faucet in the centre, so we each lean against an end and put our feet up on the sides. He's lit several candles, and it's beautiful soaking with him in the fiery light. I notice how gratifyingly little water I displace now; if I sit up and lie back down, the level barely changes.

We don't say much. I just feel his presence flowing towards me, so strongly at one point that I grab on to his foot beside me to steady myself in its force.

The sole of his foot feels weird, and he yanks it violently from my grip.

'What?'

'Don't touch my feet.'

'Okay.' He sets it carefully back on the edge, a little further away from me now. 'Why?'

'Just don't touch them.'

The water feels different now, agitated. I wait a while, and when he relaxes again I lean back a little further so I can get a look at his sole. It's messed up. Scar tissue, skin graft, something like that. His eyes are closed. I look at the other foot, and see its matching massacred flesh.

* * *

In bed when he kisses me his lips send off an electric shock and I feel the burn of this miniature attack for a prolonged moment. He blindfolds me again, and the thing about that is it does heighten my other senses. I hear his busy hands on the rope, his elevated heart-beat, and outside, a large boat sloshes water carelessly against the banks, and the staccato argument of a man and a woman grows louder and then more distant before it disappears. As he lifts my head and slides the noose over it, I smell my own arousal. Then the friction of rope around bedpost, connecting with the tightening rope around my neck. Feeling the shape of him bit by bit as he enters me, and then the friction of him, the almost unbearable pleasure of it, my seeping walls, the gradual constriction of my throat, and the mouth to mouth, only instead of giving me more air, he's taking more away, filling my mouth hole with his tongue, the delicate flicker of the intricate muscles of it, and then I'm moving at a speed that I've never felt, never felt possible. The universe has a hole, a beautiful hole that looks like it's made of meteor showers or zillions of simultaneously shooting stars, or tumbling diamonds.

* * *

The sunlight has a vice grip on my head, I feel my heartbeat in my throat, and if I were to smell any food right now I would definitely vomit. The traffic from the street below shudders through the mattress.

'Good morning,' I hear. Just to the right of the bombardment of light pounding through the window, Majid sits in a chair putting on his shoes, and I remember his feet, and feet are the only parts of our body that need special armour. So vulnerable are they, the part of us that has the job of carrying our weight in our contact with the world, that most of the terrain they negotiate would be too painful and threatening without a manufactured buffer, of wood or leather or rubber or cork. Majid's shoes have black calfskin uppers with a capped toe, and a thick, smooth tan leather sole, discoloured in the weight-laden spots by Paris's filth.

'What happened to your feet?'

He ties his laces tightly. 'I'm going to the studio for a

little while. I'll be back this afternoon. What are you going to do today?'

I have no desire to get out of bed. 'I don't know.'

He kisses my forehead. 'I charged your mobile. Would you please let me know where you are if you go off somewhere?'

The scars are mostly on the soft arch, the non-weight-supporting part that avoids touching the ground. An arch, a bridge, shelter.

He hands me my phone. 'Okay?'

'Okay.' I grab him and kiss him hard on his soft lips, and he lingers for a moment, touching my hair, which does not fall out, before he walks off in his beautiful shoes on his beaten feet.

I spend the afternoon at an internet café reading about torture. I don't want to use his computer. He might detect my search.

The prison: Evin. The techniques: Beating people on the soles of their feet with electric cables. The feet become so swollen that the victim's shoe size changes, often several sizes. Firing squads. Mass hangings. Marching blindfolded prisoners through rows of hanging bodies. Or, sometimes, the guards would put a noose around the neck of a blindfolded prisoner, put the prisoner up on a block or chair, and just let them stand there in agony, sure that they were about to die, and then arbitrarily release them.

I touch my own neck, feel its fluttering pulse. I shut down the computer, watch the words disappear, and bolt out of the place, slapping a ten-euro note on the front counter. I make it to the kerb, at least, before I throw up.

* * *

'My love,' he says, mellow-voiced. A beautiful way to be greeted.

He's sitting on the low couch smoking hash. His eyelids are at half mast. Persian music emanates from the speakers, the santur, the tar, quavering.

'Hi.' I just stand there, looking at him, unable to move. Unable to look at him without seeing the horror of what must have happened to him. I can't get the images out of my head.

He takes me by the arm and pulls me down next to him. One tender kiss on the lips and then he offers me the hash pipe, from which I inhale deeply, several times, and the images slowly fold themselves up.

We lie back and listen to the music for a while, and I'm getting little rushes as I stare at the intricate jewel-toned patterns on the rug. I smoke two cigarettes and then he says, 'Pomegranate sharbat.'

'What?'

'I used to sit in the garden, and my mother would

bring me pomegranate sharbat. I would let it melt on my tongue.' He speaks very slowly, as if he's writing the words with his tongue. 'In the garden there were almond trees with white blossoms, and jasmine trees. The smell of the jasmine was paradise. Paradise. *Pari-deiza*. It means "walled garden".' He closes his eyes. 'My mother was very beautiful. She had long, shining black hair, high cheek-bones, and liquid, almond-shaped eyes. At parties in our house she loved to dance.' Traces of a smile disappear from his face. 'My father had two wives.'

'At the same time?'

'On ne peut pas partager l'amour.' He opens his eyes again and looks at me with pupil-filled irises. He takes my hand in his, which is unusually cold. 'Delam barayeh shoma tang meshovad.'

'What does that mean?'

'It means . . .' he clasps our hands to his chest '. . . it means something like, "My heart likes to have you here."'

I feel the beat of his hand, faintly, in mine. Transla-tions are never quite complete, and I wish I could say these words, know these words, in their fullest sense. 'My heart likes to have you here, too.'

He kisses me, and I don't know how long the expanding

kiss goes on, and then he has the scarf in his hands, the blindfold, that he lifts to my head and ties tightly over my eyes.

Blindfolded prisoners, marched through rows of hanging bodies, bumping into them, not knowing what they are, at first, not until they grab on to the hanging legs to avoid losing balance.

I don't think I can do this. I try to take off the blindfold, but he grabs me by the wrists, twists my arms behind my back, and I struggle to break loose from his grip, but I'm powerless in this position. He ties my hands together. My heart starts beating wildly, and I twist around, and he thinks I'm really into it, and I'm scared.

My body and my brain begin to move on separate planes. Behind the blindfold, the images unfold, and I see him, unsteady on his damaged feet, stumbling against a dangling body, maybe the body of a friend, a teacher, an uncle, catching his fall with the shock of their cold legs.

And then I feel the warmth of him inside me, and my body betrays me, my wetness masking my horror. The noose is next, and when I try to cry out, no sound emerges, and it's tightening, constricting, and he's pushing harder into me.

I can't move, I can't see, I can't speak. I wait for it to be over.

I think about Ben Ho braiding my hair, running his fingernails along my scalp to separate my hair into three sections. He's good at braiding, having learned on ponies' manes, and his hands are very sure, the braid nicely secure, but not too tight.

We're eleven years old, and it's a perfect fall Saturday, and we take our ponies for a ride in the psychedelic woods, the red, gold and orange of the leaves so deeply bright that they look like they're vibrating. There's a chill in the air, but the sun is blazing, and Pete, my pony, feels bouncy with excitement, and he lets out a happy snort. Ben Ho and his pony are right beside us. I feel the comforting weight of my rope of hair hanging down my back. Ben Ho and I bring our ponies into a trot. We ride through a swirl of golden leaves.

We round a corner and come upon a huge turkey vulture, its ugly red face immersed in some unrecognizable form of carrion, but when the vulture sees us, it lets out something between a hiss, a scream and amp feedback. Pete freaks out. He bolts.

There's nothing much I can do except keep my weight

in the stirrups and hang on for the ride. I know that Ben Ho can't come after me, because that would just get Pete racing more. We're flying along the trail, and ahead I see a fallen tree and I know we're going over it, and Pete sails cleanly, and there's something exhilarating about being out of control. Pete is no longer a trained animal, he is pure adrenalin-fuelled motion, he is wild.

But then he begins to settle down, and I calm him through my legs, and we stop to wait for Ben Ho. I hear the crunch of leaves as he rides steadily towards me.

I feel Majid's body finally go slack.

* * *

He removes the blindfold. The blindfold is wet. He looks at me, stunned. 'You were crying?'

I didn't even know that I had been. 'I guess so.'

'Why?'

My body feels so leaden that I can't move. I can't sit up and look at him.

'Why were you crying?' He sounds agitated. I see his hand swipe at his cigarette pack on the coffee table. The veins on his hand are standing out more than usual, as if there is more blood running through them.

'Can I have a spoonful of poppies?'

I hear the click of his lighter, smell the smoke of his long exhalation. 'Tell me.'

I really, really want that spoonful, the whooshblam into my brain, the phewahhhhhh relief of it absorbing into my bloodstream. 'May I please have the spoonful first?' Manners. Manners are very important.

He has a few more silent puffs, and then he goes into the bathroom. It seems like a very long wait before he comes back with the phial. I prop myself up with a red silk pillow against the bolster, and he tilts the spoon to my nose.

I wait for the horrible leaden feeling to go away, and suddenly there's a sensation of being lifted, and I'm lifted right up out of my body, so words can come out of my mouth now, and I watch them, like cartoon bubbles blown from my lips.

'I can't do that any more.'

'What can't you do?'

'Wear the blindfold. The noose.'

'You like that. You've always liked that.' There are pretty beads of sweat above his upper lip.

'I don't like it any more.'

'You seemed to me to be . . . responding.' I see him slide two fingers into me, slide them back out, and then his fingers go right to where those beads of sweat are. He closes his eyes, inhales deeply.

'I know, but in my head, the things I'm seeing in my head, I don't want to see them.'

His eyes snap open. 'What things?' The veins at his temples are two writhing purple serpents trapped underneath his skin.

'I did some research on Evin.'

I see the purple serpents slither down the sides of his face and feel them each coil around my neck, and, with their two heads facing each other, they begin to squeeze uniformly with their long, smooth muscles. This is what was supposed to be. I was supposed to die, but the obstetrician interfered, snipping my death away from me. I hate him for it. I could have hitched a ride and been a sort of remora soul, hosted by Ben Ho.

Majid seems far away, very far, with his mouth shaping words that don't reach me, and I feel like I'm looking at him through a lens. I hold my hands up to my right eye and frame him, closing my left eye, viewing him like this, and he zooms into focus, an extreme close-up.

I watch a blood vessel burst in the white of his eye. His hand is outside of my focus, so the ear-ringing whack on the side of my head is a shock, but still, I keep looking.

I see in his burst eye that he isn't here in this room, maybe he's in a room with surging voltage, being electrically beaten, and that room will always be inside him and I will never truly understand his pain. To use the phrase 'a tortured soul' or 'tortured artist' is a horrible insult, a diminishment, to the literally tortured.

He's yelling at me in Farsi. So many sounds coming from his throat: the gurgling 'h's, the percolating vowels. He is foreign to me in every way. Everyone in the world is foreign to me, aliens all, except Ben Ho.

Majid's fluid drips down the inside of my right thigh. I don't want to have a body any more. He pulls my hands away from my face and holds my wrists together.

Many things . . . are happening to my body.

It hurts.

Stops.

He hurls my clothes at me.

My belt buckle hits my cheek.

'Get out,' he says.

While I get dressed, he's wailing and punching the

wall until his blood is running down it in knuckle-spaced rivulets.

I pocket the phial and grab my purse. He doesn't look at me as I slip out the door. I pull it shut. Heavy door. I can't hear him any more.

I think my asshole is bleeding.

* * *

Remember where I am. Think taxi stand. Head that way.

Until barricades. Police. I'm blocked by a parade.

Drawn swords flashing in the slanted sunlight. Onlooking faces reflected in Roman-centurion-style helmets. Red brush trim scratching at the sky.

I turn away, my steps out of synch with the beating drums.

* * *

In the quiet of the cab I listen to the high-pitched ringing of my left ear. It's the sort of sound that electrical currents make, coursing through cords.

I don't think I'm bleeding any more, but I'm glad my jeans are dark.

Triumphant architecture scrolls by the windows,

slipping away. Bodies scurry, faces blur. When the buildings slow down and the taxi stops, there is just the red door with the seven on it.

Inside my pocket is the small miracle of the weight of my keys. I unlock the door, and as soon as I enter the passageway to the courtyard I know that Ben Ho is here.

I pause before the dizzying stairs. The banister is rope, and I pull myself upwards, my own steps, I know, incrementally thinning the marble in the centre of each stair. The marble that is worn away, bit by bit, where do these bits go?

*   *   *

I ingest his smell. Little colliding pieces of him travel high up my nose and then curve down into my throat.

And then his sound waves enter me. 'Hey.' And then, 'Are you tripping, or what? Your eyes look strange.'

Ben Ho is sitting on the floor sorting through a case, its interior red, of antique surgical instruments. Saws and hammers for the carpentry; scissors, needles and hooks for the sewing. He arranges and rearranges the various implements. One mysterious item has three small hooks connected by delicate chains. The saw handle looks like the butt of a revolver. Its teeth have chewed through many bones. He lines up a row of scalpels, their blades of graduating lengths. Finally he uncoils his limbs and approaches me, looking at me with those steady, steady eyes. I don't cry.

We embrace. I suck in more of his molecules. He touches my hair.

'Your hair's all tangled. You want me to brush it out?'

All I can manage is a nod.

The only brush in the apartment now is part of a set of tarnished silver men's brushes, their boar bristles militaristically stiff. I sit down on the golden bumblebee cushion and wait. He starts from the ends, working his way gently up towards the roots. So many years of hair.

'Remember how you used to lie on the glass coffee table and press your face against it, so your nose and mouth would be all smushed, and I'd lie underneath the table and laugh?'

'Yeah, I was an expert at making you laugh. You used to laugh so hard that your laughter was silent.' He's reached the top of my scalp. 'So, what's going on? You seem freaked out.'

His words to me not easily delivered, like he's trying to make them sound. His pitch is higher and his voice almost breaks, and I wonder if he sees the four little red rivers, gently streaming down the wall, or if he feels things happening to my body, smells violation. He begins to braid my hair.

'And do you remember when we were out in the backyard with our bubble wands, the ones that made those giant bubbles, and then Graham brought us the dead baby rabbit?'

'I remember,' he says. His fingernail scrapes a line down my scalp. 'It was the first time I'd touched anything dead. Just an inanimate bunny-shaped sack of fur.'

'But Graham didn't really kill it.'

'No, he's a bird dog. His mouth was very gentle.'

'The rabbit's body was totally unharmed.'

'He didn't have to die. He died –'

'Of fear.'

'I was, sort of, mad at the rabbit for that. He could have survived.'

'But fear was part of the bunny. A survival mechanism.'

'It backfired.'

'In this case.'

The braid is finished. Ben Ho pulls it over my shoulder. 'Here. Hold the end for me.'

I clamp my fingers down on it. The end looks like a blonde paintbrush. He cuts a piece of surgical gauze and secures the braid with it.

'Your hands are shaking,' I say.

They shake worse as he lights a cigarette. He studies me. Maybe he's going to do my portrait. His hands settle down.

'I'm going to have to take you to the hospital.'

'The hospital? What are you talking about?'

'You're – not well.'

'No fucking way. Hospitals are like prisons.' I light a cigarette, too. We face each other and blow duelling clouds of smoke.

'You need to eat.'

'I'll eat.'

'Sure. Two tiny nibbles of a cheese sandwich.'

'I'll eat right now. A feast. You can watch me.'

He stubs out his cigarette. 'A feast, eh? All right. Where do you want to go?'

'I don't want to go out. I have a chill. I need to take a bath. Can you go out and get stuff?'

He sighs. 'What do you want?'

'Roast chicken and potatoes au gratin and caviar and champagne and millefeuille pastries.'

He puts on his jacket. There's a pale blue paint stain on the cuff. 'Well, I don't know about that, but I'll see what I can find. I'm hungry, too.'

We kiss on the lips. His are smooth, warm and fleshy, and I still feel them pressed softly against mine when he leaves.

★ ★ ★

I take the phial from my pocket and examine it. A fresh supply, completely full. It is enough.

I choose a very sharp pair of scissors and cut off my braid to leave for him.

Paper. A charcoal pencil, so the writing will be dust that will blur and fade. Only 'I love you.' What else? There is nothing else. *Au revoir*? No. *Auf wiedersehen*? No. 'Auf wiedersein.'

I want to be clean. In the bathtub I inhale all of it. The powder follows Ben Ho's molecules up my nasal passageways and then begins its descent. I turn the spigot off and lie down. Float.

Just beneath the surface of the cold, clear ocean, thousands of large sea creatures are swimming in unison; sharks, swordfish, barracudas, muscular fish, silver-flecked, and I'm swimming with them, and though I have the thought that I could be severed or stung, I don't have the fear. I'm just part of this school moving powerfully through the deep swells of water, through the ocean's rhythm. The creatures, menacing and beautiful, keep swimming, swiftly, with mysterious purpose.

And I feel the tentacled creature inside me slipping out of my body as I glide forwards. A millipus, its head shooting out first, the thousand tentacles streaming after it. Then it wraps one tentacle at a time around me, around my arms, my legs, my body, my head, cradling me as it takes me into the deep.

Acknowledgements

Many thanks to: Simon Prosser and Anna Kelly for their editing and enthusiasm; Sarah Coward for her meticulous copy-editing, and to all the staff at Penguin UK who worked on this book; Adam Pincus, Suzanne Myers, Kyle Hamlett and Kelli Shay Hix for their early reads; Reza Moini for his very generous help with my research on Iran; Dr Mary Gingrass and Dr Blake for their expert advice; Dr Ari Babakian and Elena Rohrmoser for their help with translations, and Richard Espenant for consultation on fine points in French grammar; Isabelle Townsend, Patrick Deedes-Vincke, Salah Kliti, Karin Eaton, Pamela Huson, Carlyon Allan, Guinevere van Seenus, Karolina Kurkova, Carmen Kass, Tillman von Lauterbach, Richard Sinott, Natasha Fraser-Cavassoni and Laure de Gramont for their stories and aid in researching the fashion world; Tom Calder, Lisa Froeb and Zack Spiger for their friendship and support; Tarquin Callen and Marjorie Jones for their kind hospitality, comfort and support; Erich Vogel for his photo; Paul Boche for his poem; and Tyler Zwiep for the inspiration of his drawings.